ALWAYS IVETTE

ALWAYS IVETTE

SYDNEY WINWARD

This is a work of fiction. Names, characters, places, and incidents are either the product of the author's imagination or are used fictitiously, and any resemblance to actual persons living or dead, business establishments, events, or locales, is entirely coincidental.

Always, Ivette

To all the fairy tales I read as a child

BOOKS BY SYDNEY WINWARD

The Bloodborn Series

Bloodborn

Bloodbond

Bloodscourge

Bloodbane

Bloodcurse

Sunlight and Shadows Series

A Breath of Sunlight

A Taste of Shadows

A Glimpse of Music

A Kiss of Embers

Letters to Love Series

Yours, Sterling

Forever, Mirabelle

Always, Ivette

Lord Death Series

A Waltz with Lord Death

Novellas

Through Wylder Meadows

Root Brew Float

On Silver Wings

Bloodmoon

Selkie

Chapter One

On one's birthday, one should be celebrating, not scouring the countryside in the middle of a blistering storm with no sign of civilization within several leagues. Alone and soaked to the bone with nothing but his horse and his own mind to keep him company.

Barnaby Mavis scowled at the sprawling green fields where the Danvers residence was supposed to reside. But nothing stood out aside from tall trees, long fields, and a cluster of sheep huddled together for warmth as rain tumbled down from gray clouds.

Seething through his teeth, he mumbled to himself, "Where there are sheep, there must be a master."

He clicked his tongue, and his mount obeyed the order to continue forward along the slick grass, whipping its tail in agitation at having to travel through the storm.

"You and me both." He patted the horse's shoulder to try to calm him. But he recognized the way the creature straddled the fine edge of calm and terror. They would seek shelter in the nearby town of Avorstead.

As soon as this blasted deal was over and done with.

Prince Sterling had tasked him with paying back every coin he'd unknowingly swindled from desperate folks in the form of loans. The loans had been legal. But the interest rates had been far too high after the cap on the rate amidst the economic crash in Edilann.

His heart sank to the pits of his stomach moments before he forced it back up and clenched his fists around the reins. All his life, Barnaby had thought his father a good and honest man. He'd looked up to him. Respected him. At least until months ago when he'd taken a blow to his pride, his reputation, and his character for the father who was ten months dead and left him to deal with the aftermath of his deception.

He hadn't known about the illegal interest rates. But he certainly had taken the responsibility and the tongue thrashing from more than one person, including the prince.

He reflexively gripped the ring circling his pinky beneath his black leather glove. As the horse crossed the long field, he pulled his glove off to reveal the red gemstone glinting beneath the dark clouds overhead. Rain sprinkled over its smooth-cut surface, giving it a sheen clear enough to show a glimmer of his reflection.

He scowled at the man staring back at him in the tiny facet of the gem. The man he hated with every fiber of his being. Not only did his blond hair and blue eyes look remarkably similar to his father's, but the hardness in his eyes, the rigidness of his shoulders, the set of his jaw reminded him of the father who had betrayed him and left him to suffer the consequences.

He tore off the ring and threw it with all his might, watching as the small piece of jewelry arced through the air and struck the trunk of a tree with a *tink!*

It plopped into the grass, hidden from view.

Rain continued to pour from the skies as he led the horse around the sheep and toward the small cliffside blocked by a wooden fence. If he could figure out where he was from the high ground, he may be able to spot the village yet.

Each step the horse took across the slippery terrain echoed the shallow beats of his heart. He slipped his pocket watch from the breast pocket of his vest and gazed somberly at the ornate designs etched into the gold metal. For a brief moment, he glimpsed parties, drinking, laughter, and women in his mind.

But one woman in particular…

Mirabelle Waters with her dark hair and her hazel eyes and her short stature. He'd treated her terribly. Said horrible things he never should have said. Under the influence of liquor, he was…out of control. Of his thoughts. Of his actions. And he despised himself for it.

A shiver trembled down his spine as he swiped water from his cheeks. Yes, it was *rainwater*, because lords never cried lest they endure a great mocking and belittlement from everyone around them.

Lightning flashed across the sky, lighting up the area around him.

The horse nickered, flattening his ears back against his head.

"Keep going," he said, patting the horse's shoulder once more as they neared the wooden fence. He slipped the pocket watch into his trousers' pocket instead, grateful to hide the memories away once more. "Almost there."

Another flash of light lit up the sky, followed by distant thunder. He squinted against the brightness as an unbearable headache claimed every inch of his head and face. One week sober was literal torture. His head ached. His body felt sluggish. His mind screamed for just a little sip.

But he no longer wanted to allow something else to control him. He wanted to control himself.

Which was why he'd decided to go on this blasted quest in search of the Danvers family. If he was missing on the one day he was socially expected to drink and dance and woo women, no one could pressure him into giving into the drink.

He reined his horse back a good few paces from the fence and peered over the side of the cliff. His heart skipped with relief when he noticed the field sloped downward into another stretch of field, which led to a lone cottage tucked against a dirt road. Flickers of lantern light lit up the windows, warm and inviting and filled with actual people rather than livestock.

His gaze followed the dirt road next to the house, and it led to several other houses next to large fields before tapering into a small town with a cluster of houses and buildings nearly hidden beneath the haze of rain falling in sheets from the sky.

Avorstead.

"So close now. We're almost there."

But this time the lightning gave no warning as a blinding flash lit up the sky, and thunder boomed directly over their heads. His mount whinnied and reared up. He clung to the saddle while trying to seize control of the horse with the reins.

"Whoa, boy. Whoa!"

The hooves hit the ground with a jarring thud, nearly sending him toppling over the side of the saddle. He gripped the reins again and tried to turn the horse toward the hill leading to the cottage. But it only spun around and backed up, fighting the reins, until its rear end brushed against the wooden fence overlooking the cliff.

Barnaby's heart jumped to his throat as he attempted to dismount, but the horse shifted until his leg was pinned between the creature's body and the fence post.

Rather than keeping the reins tight with control, he allowed them to go slack in his hands to encourage the horse to move. But it only threw its head back and ripped the reins from his hands entirely before it thrashed its head and backed up farther until the fence creaked from its weight.

"Go!" he shouted, glancing with terror from the slick grass to the steep drop over the cliffside. He kicked the horse's flank with his free foot. His mount moved just enough for him to free his second foot.

But another crash of thunder smashed into the skies like a hammer to a mirror directly above them. The hairs on his arms stood up. The horse didn't only rear this time, but it started bucking like a frantic animal trapped in a cage of lightning.

Get off, get off, get off! he shouted silently to himself. But he could do nothing more than hold on with a vice-like grip as his body was jerked violently with each buck.

With one last kick of its legs, the horse flung him off its back. His feet touched solid ground for mere moments before the momentum caused him to crash into the wooden fence.

The wood splintered.

He screamed.

And then he fell from the cliffside with one last flash of lightning as the backdrop to his vision before his body smashed against the ground.

And his world turned black.

Chapter Two

Yvette Danvers' shout was swallowed by roaring thunder and pouring rain. Her eyes widened with horror as someone fell from the cliffside on the hill. And they didn't get back up.

"Mercy!" she breathed as she kicked her horse into a canter. The creature was used to loud noises and didn't spook easily, even amidst a raging storm.

From this distance, she couldn't tell whether the fallen rider was a man, woman, or child, only that they lay in a heap and didn't move. The horse at the top of the hill galloped away, abandoning its rider to their unfortunate fate.

She slowed her horse to a trot, and then to a walk before she slid off the wet saddle and landed in damp grass with a *squelch* of her boots. She picked up her skirts and rushed toward the unconscious figure lying at the base of the cliff.

Ice squeezed her heart when she found a man's body tangled among fallen branches and jutting rocks. Dark red blood oozed from beneath blond hair matted to his forehead and cheek. An arm was twisted at an impossible angle. And his skin was far too pale for her liking.

Kneeling at his side, she unbuttoned his coat and pushed open his vest with the attempt to locate his heartbeat, only to inhale sharply at the blood soaked into the clothing at his side.

Her hand flew to her mouth as she stifled a horrified gasp. Her hands trembled as she reached for him a second time and placed her palm over his heart, searching for a sign of life. His heart beat in a weak but steady rhythm.

"Brith!" she called to her horse, and the creature's ears picked up at the sound of her name. With sure steps, Brith approached and snorted, leaning her head down to sniff the man's boot.

Ivette wasted no time as she unlatched a damp blanket from the saddle and tied one of the ends to the pommel. The blanket wasn't large by any means, but it would do the job.

At least she hoped.

Rain pelted her with its relentless drops, and thunder rolled across the sky, but thankfully, Brith held still as she worked. Ivette cursed her trembling hands as she carefully snaked her arms beneath the man's shoulders and dragged him onto the blanket. A sob escaped her when blood dripped from his head, coating her sleeves, skirts, and the blanket.

"Please hold," she begged the thin material as she urged Brith forward.

The sheet became taut and groaned at the seams, but it otherwise held as the makeshift transport dragged the bleeding man toward her home across the field.

She remained at the horse's front to guide her forward by the reins, not only to prevent her from moving too fast, but also to keep her from galloping off to the barn for warmth and shelter.

She kept a continuous eye on the man to make sure he didn't fall off the blanket. First, his boot slipped off and dragged across the damp grass. Then his lower leg. By the time they neared the house, only his upper half remained on the blanket. But it was enough.

"Senna! Lily!" she screamed for two of her four sisters.

They burst out of the house and stilled immediately when their gazes fell on the wounded man. But they didn't hesitate to follow her orders as she instructed them to make up a quick bed on the floor for him. Together, the three of them dragged him into the front room and onto a pile of blankets. Blood quickly soaked into the threads, but she didn't spare a thought for them when a man's life was in danger.

Although they didn't own much, Senna brought her a pile of rags while Lily entered the room with a bucket of water.

Blood smeared across Ivette's hands, arms, and clothing as she cleaned the head wound as quickly as her shaking hands allowed. And then she wrapped the wound tight to staunch the bleeding.

Next, she shimmied him out of his coat, vest, and shirt, only to face a gruesome wound on his side. A sharp branch was buried into his skin, broken off as if it had snapped under the duress of his weight.

Lily, with her fragile disposition, rushed outside only to vomit into the bushes. Thankfully, Senna kept their two youngest sisters from entering the room, and instead sent them to the stables with the horse to unsaddle her and brush her down.

Ivette took a knife from Senna's hand and used it to carefully dig out the splinters from the bleeding wound. It worried her when the man didn't stir nor protest to any degree as she thoroughly cleaned the wound with the knife, and even after pouring alcohol over the injury.

Still no movement from him.

She kept glancing at his face as she bound his side with strips of cloth. His chest rose and fell with each breath. But he remained unconscious.

"Do you think it's broken?" Senna nodded her head toward the man's arm.

She bit her lip, noting the way the bottom of his elbow extended farther than his bicep. "I'm not a physician." Nor could they afford one. They were barely keeping afloat as it was.

Still, she gently rested his arm in her hands and felt along the bones. Nothing seemed amiss aside from his elbow. Possibly dislocated. But she needed a man to help her lodge it back into its socket.

"How is he still alive?" Senna clutched her hands to her chest as she stared at him. Not just at his injuries, but at his face. Yes, he was a *very* good-looking man. Even covered in blood and wrapped in bandages, his face as pale as the cream gathered at the top of fresh milk.

Ivette frowned and busied herself with bundling his soiled clothing together with the intent of washing them. "A fall from that height could have killed him. He's lucky to be alive."

And it was lucky she had been outside at the time in the storm, checking on the sheep. She never would have seen him otherwise.

Next, she carefully pulled the soiled blankets from beneath him and replaced them with new ones free of blood, maneuvering his body one way and then the other to tuck them beneath him.

Heat filled her cheeks upon placing her hands on the bare skin of his torso. The muscles were firm against her touch, with broad shoulders and a narrow waist. No hair marred his smooth chest, and his physique was that of someone who took great care in their appearance. She couldn't tell how old he was, especially when a bandage covered nearly half his face. But she placed him somewhere near her own age of twenty-four.

"Watch over him for a minute," she told her sister. "I'll fetch the neighbor to help with his arm."

Without waiting for her answer, Ivette stepped outside into the lingering cold of a storm moving past their fields. She took a moment to breathe in the fresh air, leaning against the side of the cottage to gather her emotions. Her copper hair was matted, and she grimaced when she realized it was coated in blood.

Being the eldest of five sisters was not for the faint of heart. But even she struggled with the sight of so much blood, with the possibility that a man might still die on their property, and she didn't have the funds to bring a physician to him.

After inhaling one last deep breath, she dumped the bloodied clothing and blankets into an outdoor wash bin filled with rainwater. Unfortunately, her sisters were already putting Brith back into the barn, which forced her to walk the distance to their next-door neighbor's house.

Her somewhat dried skirts now soaked up mud all over again as she trekked down the lane leading to the dirt road.

She hugged the side of the path while avoiding the ditch until she spotted the silhouette of the Keswick's house in the waxing darkness.

Her boots slipped in mud puddles. The bite of the chill stung her bones. And she only just realized she was still covered in blood by the time she knocked on the Keswick's door.

Elinor opened the door and released a startled gasp, her hand flying to her large, round belly. "What happened to you, dear?"

She tried to usher her inside, but Ivette shook her head. "The blood isn't mine."

The woman's face paled. "One of your sisters?"

Again, she shook her head, teeth chattering. "A man fell from the cliffside in our field. Is Vincent home? I need his help."

The screaming of children brought her attention to the inside of their home as three young boys ran amuck as they chased each other around, completely oblivious to the open door.

A moment later, Vincent stood in the doorway, also bombarding her with question after question until he slipped his boots and coat on and followed her back to her home. The time he served in the army was apparent in the way he held his body with confidence, in the way his gaze swept the path ahead, in the way he kept one hand on his belt where a sword may have once resided. If anyone knew how to fix the mysterious man's arm, it was him.

Finally, they reached her home where her sisters huddled together in the kitchen next to the main room, eyes wide as they kept stealing glances toward the injured man.

Ivette wasn't sure what they were more intimidated by—blood or the man's handsome face.

Besides, most of the blood was gone.

"By the bellows of autumntide," Vincent muttered under his breath as he slipped his boots off and left them beside the door. "He's on death's doorstep."

Lily burst into tears, and Senna quickly pulled her into an embrace to allow her to sob into her shoulder.

"Mind your words," Ivette hissed.

Vincent grimaced apologetically. "I have boys. I'm not used to having to tiptoe around feelings."

He took one look at the injured man's arm and his expression turned serious as if he'd stepped on a battlefield filled with injured men rather than into a home with only one wounded man.

He instructed her to hold the man's forearm steady, and in a quick movement, he popped the elbow back into the joint.

The injured man grimaced but remained unconscious as Vincent tied the arm into a sling. A smidge of relief filled her at the small sign of life. Surely, he would be just fine.

Surely.

"Do you know who he is?" Ivette asked, wringing her hands together. The sooner they could get in contact with a family member, the better.

Vincent didn't answer immediately. Instead, he rummaged through the pockets of the man's trousers. A long, golden chain pulled from the man's pocket, attached to an ornate, circular pocket watch.

He shook his head as he opened the golden case to inspect it before handing it to her next. The initials B.A.M. stared back at her, engraved on the back. "I don't know who he is, but he's filthy rich with his watch and fancy clothes. Gotta be."

Ivette snapped her head toward the man. Hope alighted in her chest, followed by worry when his face seemed to have gotten paler in the last hour. If he survived his injuries, perhaps he might repay them for their kindness by helping them out of their perilous financial situation.

"I'll have Elinor pack up a pot of broth for you. Probably could use it. What else can we do for you? I would take him myself but…best not to move him."

She shook her head and hugged her arms tight around her torso. "This is not the first time we've had to do this. We'll be alright."

The man gave her a look of sympathy before he pulled on his shoes and slipped back outside into the night. And when she returned her attention to the injured man, she found her youngest sister, Helen, tucking more blankets around him when he started shivering. Senna lit a fire in the hearth, and together, the five of them stared at him for far too long.

"What do we do with him?" Senna asked, breaking the uncertain silence inside the cottage.

The firelight cast flickers of shadows across his face and chest, reminding her she needed to wash and dry his clothing so he could wear them as soon as possible.

"We take it one day at a time," she declared with a confidence she didn't feel.

But if this man could save her family, she would do everything in her power to make sure he lived.

The light of morning seared Ivette's eyelids.

She groaned as she blinked back the unwanted intrusion. A crick in her neck protested against the movement as she lifted her head. Only for her to groan again when she found her arms folded over the wash bin where she must have fallen asleep late in the night.

An imprint of the wood created a mark on her arms, the sleeves folded up to her elbows. Her back ached from sleeping in such an uncomfortable position.

When had she fallen asleep? Before or after she washed the clothing?

Her gaze lifted to the clothesline above her head, only to sigh in relief to find the mystery man's clothes pinned and drying beneath the morning breeze.

A blanket lay over her shoulders, which must have protected her from the chill as she'd worked. There had been *so much* blood... She'd had no choice but to dump out the water and fill the bucket three times until the last wash left no speck of red.

Of course, her sisters had helped where they could... But she'd wanted to spare them of the ghastly sight. Just like she'd spared them from the extent of their mother's injuries...

She shook the heartbreaking memories from her mind and stood from the creaking wooden stool, blinking several more times until her eyes adjusted to the bright light. The damp grass sprawled out before her on fields well-manicured from grazing sheep. A small apple orchard rested to the right of the house while a barn lay on the left.

Several sheep bleated their greeting from where they grazed in the nearby field, huddled together once again.

Taking a deep breath, she forced her stiff legs to move toward the line. She pinched the man's vest between her fingers. Still damp. But the white shirt was completely dry. At least he'd have something to wear to maintain some decency in a house filled with young women.

She plucked the shirt off the line and ventured indoors. But then her mouth pinched with worry when she found little Helen kneeling at the man's unconscious side, staring intently at him as if searching for something.

"He's still breathing," Helen said before she stood and skipped toward her, copper hair flying behind her in her wake. "Vincent was wrong. He's not going to die."

Grace entered the house from the kitchen entrance with a pail filled with milk. Like usual, she said nothing, preferring to keep quiet and keep to herself.

For all her life, she'd called her "sister," the two of them eight years apart. But the girl's dark brown hair and dark eyes made her suspect her mother might have had an affair. Her parents' marriage had been an unhappy one, especially when her father had taken all their money and ran off with another woman.

But they were all sisters through and through, no matter their parentage.

"Has he woken yet?" Ivette asked Senna where she sat at the table braiding Lily's hair.

Her sister shook her head. "Only whimpers. I suspect he's in a great deal of pain."

"I imagine so."

She snatched folded white linens from the table and knelt beside the man, noting the way her sisters also moved closer, some sitting on nearby chairs, others hovering close by.

She loved her sisters. She truly did. But every once in a while, she wished they would give her a little space. Especially now as she tended to a half-naked man.

Not wanting to disturb his arm too much, she slipped it out of the sling and carefully maneuvered it through one of the sleeves of his white shirt. She wrapped it around his back and tucked the other arm through as well before buttoning it all the way to the top so no skin showed except his neck.

When she finished tying the sling over his shoulder, she shifted her attention to the bandage at his head.

Slowly, she unwrapped it to avoid jostling the injury, and when the white cloth fell away from his face…

They let out a collective gasp.

Not at his injury and the blood soaked into the bandage. But because his dry blond hair wisped over his forehead in an elegant swoop. Because his straight nose led down to attractive lips. Because his flawless skin was now filled with color when it had been lacking entirely last night.

"He's…*beautiful*!" Senna exclaimed as she reached out to touch a lock of his blond hair.

"Stop," Ivette warned, slapping her hand away. "He's injured."

But her younger sister paid no heed as she sat in a chair facing backward, resting her chin on her folded arms as she continued to stare at him. "Do you think he's married?"

Both of them glanced toward his ring finger at the same time, only to find it bare. But it didn't necessarily mean he was unattached. And although the man was absurdly handsome, they knew nothing about him. Not even his name. He could be a thief for all they knew. Or a mercenary. Perhaps even a murderer.

Yet, the clothing he wore was fine and velvety and tailored perfectly to his body. His hands were soft and free of hard calluses like many men she knew. And the pocket watch they'd found in his trousers spoke of wealth and status.

Who was this strange man? And how had he ended up in their fields?

"Should we tell someone?" squeaked Grace behind them. At sixteen years old, even she wasn't immune to the man's handsome looks as she stared at his face, cheeks blushing red to bring out the dark contrast of her hair. "The town doctor ought to see him."

"We haven't the money for a doctor." Ivette's mouth pinched with worry. "We'll wait until he wakes up. I'm sure someone will come by looking for him long before then."

She tried to keep her eyes on her handiwork as she placed a folded linen against his injury and wrapped another cloth snuggly around his head once again. But she kept stealing glances at his face, and more than once, her gaze dropped to his lips, and then to the attractive Adam's apple of his throat.

"Mercy," she whispered to herself, shaking her head sternly. She could not be ogling a strange man, especially when her heart responded in a rather transparent manner. However, she couldn't help but wonder what color his eyes were and what his mouth looked like when he smiled.

When she realized she wasn't the only one ogling him, she clapped her hands and shooed her sisters away. "Give him some space. Besides, we all have work to do."

And plenty of it.

If they failed to keep up, they would lose their house, their land, their sheep, and she feared she may even lose a sister.

Chapter Three

A fire steadily built up around him, starting from his side and consuming his body as the flames licked upward to his arm. And when it reached his head, he groaned and tried to swat the fire away. But his arm refused to move. His entire body felt weighed down as if swallowed by the ocean, sinking slowly to the very depths of the sea.

The heat consumed him, growing hotter and hotter until his body thrashed from side to side. No matter how hard he tried to bat the flames away, they remained consistent as if he were trapped inside a kiln.

A sob escaped his mouth as the fire turned to unbearable pain. His head thrashed to the side, but the movement caused stinging agony to crash into his skull.

He cried out and sat up so suddenly that pain pierced him near his hip. He gasped as he attempted to clutch his side, but his arm rested in a sling, and moving it even the slightest bit sent a rush of fire through his elbow.

Gasps heaved in and out of his lungs as he frantically glanced around at his surroundings. A circular, woven rug. A low table. Chairs. An unlit fireplace.

Where was he? Where was he!

What sounded like a fork clattering against a plate snapped his attention to a young girl with wide eyes as she stared back at him. She rushed out of the room, slammed open the door, and shouted for someone named Ivette to come quickly.

No, no, no. He could not wait for this stranger named Ivette to come to him. He needed to leave. Fast.

He gritted his teeth through the agony of grabbing onto a chair with his uninjured arm and hoisting himself to his feet. Immediately, his surroundings spun. His ears rang. His feet stumbled. And his vision blacked out for mere moments as he lost his footing.

He scrambled to catch himself but found himself plummeting toward the floor instead. Rather than smacking his heavy head on the wood, someone grabbed him beneath the arm and slowly lowered him into a sitting position.

Fast breaths escaped him as the black dots shrouding his vision cleared enough to find himself staring back at a woman with copper hair, hazel eyes, and freckles dotting her face. Her eyes were frantic with worry. Her lips moved as she spoke, but he couldn't hear her over the ringing in his ears.

For a brief moment, terror grasped onto his heart and squeezed. His gaze passed frantically over her, trying to find familiarity in the foreign. "Where am I?" he sobbed. "Where am I?"

And why did everything hurt so blasted much?

Although his ears still rang, he caught onto the gentle caress of her voice. "You're in our home," she said, gripping his hand and squeezing. "You fell off the cliffside and sustained a few terrible injuries." Another squeeze. "You've been unconscious for days."

Days?

"No, no, no. I have to get home. I have to—"

His words cut off as his head spun, and he would have slumped over onto the floor if Ivette hadn't kept a steady hand on him.

"Shh, shh, shh," she soothed. "Take deep breaths. We'll see you home. But you need to calm yourself."

He did as instructed despite how his lungs threatened to capsize. After a few deep breaths, his heart calmed, and his head stopped spinning. Another woman who was not Ivette or the young girl approached with a cup of water and handed it to Ivette.

Embarrassment flooded his cheeks when he reached for it with a shaking hand, but only managed to slop the water onto the floor. Ivette cupped her hands around his and the cup and helped him drink. Just the simple movement caused his surroundings to spin again until his stomach threatened to retch up what he'd only moments before consumed.

"All right, now," Ivette murmured in a soothing tone. "We need to get you home to someone who can help take care of you until you heal. Where do you live?"

His mouth opened to reply, but the answer refused to come. He stared blankly at her until his brows furrowed as the effort to recall the information flitted out of reach. "I don't know."

Ivette shared a look with the girl who had handed her the water, very similar in coloring except her hair was light brown rather than copper. Her eyes were brown, whereas Ivette's were a seafoam green with a golden brown in the center.

"What's your name?" she tried again.

He growled when the frustration ate at him as he tried to recall his name. What was it? John? Jared? Angus? Edmund? "I don't know," he said again, wincing when the pain in the back of his skull pounded relentlessly like a throbbing drum. "I should know this! I fell from a cliff, you said? And hit my head it seems." He wrinkled his nose. "My name is… My name is…"

He ran a shaky hand over his chin as he tried to recall *anything*. But he remembered nothing. Not his name, where he lived, who he knew. He had no idea if he had a family or friends.

"Perhaps this might help."

She lifted a pocket watch to his eye level, opened and closed the case, and then flipped it over to reveal a set of initials on the back.

B.A.M.

Seemed fitting, as the ground had certainly given him a big whack in the back of the head.

"That's not mine."

"It was in your pocket," she pointed out. "Does your name start with 'B?'" When he stared at her blankly, she continued, "How about we call you Ben for now? Until you remember your name."

The name sounded wrong in his head. "No, that's not right."

"Bartholomew?" she ventured. "Blaine? Brock? Benedict?"

Still, none sounded right. Perhaps his name didn't start with B at all. "Ben is fine."

The second girl with the light brown hair approached with a bowl filled with wafting steam. "Are you hungry, Ben? You've been unconscious for a while."

His stomach turned at the thought of putting any food into his belly. Acid climbed his throat, and he clamped a hand over his mouth. "I think I'm going to retch."

Just as he turned to the side, Ivette was there with a bowl to catch what little water he'd consumed minutes earlier. The movement caused his head to spin and for the black wisps in his vision to return. He pitched forward as the waves of unconsciousness threatened to pull him under.

But then Ivette caught him by the shoulder, her mouth near his ear. "You need to rest. Can you help me get you back to your bed?"

"How did you get me there in the first place?" he slurred, somehow managing to get his feet beneath him while she heavily supported his weight.

"Pure fear and determination," she jested, grunting with the effort it must have taken to help lower him onto the blankets.

The moment his head lay down, his world ceased spinning, transitioning into a slow crawl before coming to a standstill. His gaze shifted from her to the four other girls standing farther behind. For a moment, he thought he might have stumbled into an only-girls school. At least until he reminded himself he was in a home, and the girls looked similar to the other.

"I'm Ivette," she said, pointing to herself. "The oldest. Next is my sister, Senna." She gestured to the water girl and then to someone with dark blonde hair and hazel eyes. "Lily comes in third, followed by Grace and then Helen."

Grace had dark brunette hair and dark brown eyes while Helen looked remarkably similar to Ivette, with copper hair but brown eyes and much younger.

None of these women looked familiar in the slightest, and he highly suspected whoever he was before the accident didn't know them either. "How did I come to be on your property? Did you see me fall?"

Helen clapped loudly, startling him enough to wince when jumping pulled on his side wound. "It was a giant thunderstorm! You looked majestic on your steed."

"Helen!" they all chided the girl at the same time.

This time, Senna spoke. "Ivette was out with the sheep. She saw you fall."

Ivette nodded. "You were riding a horse in our fields. I thought you might have gotten lost, and I turned my mount to help you. But the thunder hit directly above us. It startled your horse. It threw you into the fence, and the fence broke." She paused for a moment before lowering her voice. "There was so much blood. I thought for sure you were dead."

Ben held a hand to his aching temple when trying to recall the incident caused his head to throb. "I don't remember this at all."

"What is the last thing you *do* remember?"

Flashes of copper hair and hazel eyes burned into his memory. A face pinched with worry. Eyes frantic for his well-being. Gentle hands. A soothing voice. A beautiful face. There was something about freckles he found wholly endearing.

He shook the unexpected thought away and stared back at her like an idiot who lost all his memories and fixated on the first female face he saw.

Oh wait…

"I want to sleep," he mumbled when trying to recall anything before *her* fatigued his mind. There was no doubt about it. She'd saved his life.

"Don't wait another few days before you wake again," she warned. "Or I will dump water over your head."

"I won't," he promised sluggishly as sleep pulled him sharply into unconsciousness.

He woke what felt like hours later as something cold splashed across his face. He coughed and spluttered and shot upright into a sitting position, only to cry out when the action tugged on his wound.

Water dripped from his hair into his eyes as he stared back at Ivette with disbelief. She glared down at him, holding a bucket in her arms. "I warned you," she said in a stern tone, one hand fisted against her hip. "You've been unconscious for another three days."

"I hardly fell asleep," he protested. But the way his arm didn't hurt quite so much anymore attested to how much rest he must have gotten. His head still throbbed and his side ached, but the pain was duller in comparison to the blazing heat last he woke.

"I cannot keep spoon feeding you broth while you remain unconscious." A flicker of distress flashed across her eyes, but it disappeared quickly. "You need to eat on your own, or so help me, Ben."

He got the distinct impression from the mildew scent beneath him that this wasn't the first time she'd tried dousing him in water.

"I apologize for being a burden." He attempted to stand up, but his world spun, and he stumbled to his right. Ivette caught him around the waist and guided him toward one of the five chairs sitting around a circular dining table.

"You are not a burden," she murmured before stepping in front of the oven and checking on a loaf of bread. He watched her movements as she chopped vegetables and fruits with a knife far too dull to be safe for use. Her shoulders sagged. Her eyelids drooped. But she kept working while her sisters joined him at the table.

"Do you remember anything yet?" Senna asked, pulling his attention away from Ivette as she scooted her chair closer to him until they were a shoulder's width apart. "Your name? Your age? Your home? Your age?"

"You asked that one twice."

"Oh, I did?" Senna giggled. "Silly me."

Out of the corner of his eye, he spotted Ivette rolling her eyes as she used a paddle to retrieve the loaf of bread from the oven, and he couldn't help but grin at her reaction. Simultaneously, Senna, Lily, and Grace sighed, and his attention jumped to them, only to find each staring at his mouth.

His smile fell immediately, his eyebrows furrowing in confusion. The feeling of smug satisfaction sitting on him indicated this wasn't the first time women had swooned over his smile.

But he couldn't recall what had brought about the familiar feeling in the first place.

"Umm…" He rubbed his temple to give him a moment to think. His memory drew a blank once more, but there were things he could conclude based on observation alone. "Older than you, to be sure."

He popped open the pocket watch Ivette had found on him and stared at the golden sheen of metal catching beneath the light entering the window. He brushed a thumb across the warm metal and turned it over to view the initials on the back.

"Has anyone come looking for me?"

Lily shook her head. "We've been watching for strangers in town, but so far…no one."

"Where is 'town?'"

"Avorstead. We live in the more rural parts."

"With sheep."

"With sheep," Lily affirmed.

Ivette set a pot of broth on the table, along with bowls of vegetables and fruit and the loaf of bread. The others served themselves, and Senna even served him, but he noticed Ivette didn't take anything for herself until everyone else had their own. And when she ladled the remainder of the broth into her bowl, not much remained.

The sisters talked and chattered and laughed, completely unaware. But he noticed. And he wasn't about to let her sacrifice.

Before she could dip her bread into the broth, he reached across the table and stole her bowl, replacing it with his own. "I might retch again," he lied. "I don't have all of my appetite back."

She stared at him with surprise written in her features before she ducked her head and smiled. "If you retch, I will make you clean it up yourself next time."

"Things haven't been so bad as that."

But she simply raised an eyebrow. "Let's just say it's a good thing you've been unconscious for most of it."

Her hazel eyes lit up with mirth, and for a long few moments, he caught himself staring. But then unease twisted his stomach, and he forced his gaze away, only to frown into his bowl. He didn't know why he felt so…awful. Well, yes, he knew cracking one's head open didn't tend to go well. Ever. But something else caused the twist of discomfort. He only wished he knew what it was.

He ran a hand over his face, ignoring the looks he received as he tried to figure out what he was going to do now. Obviously, he couldn't stay here and take advantage of the kindness these girls offered. But where would he go? Especially when he was still recovering from his injuries, and he had no memories of his past life.

He could possibly find a job in town. At least until someone came in search of him. Surely, someone was out there looking for him this very second.

Despite his lie of not having an appetite, he soaked up every last drop of the broth with his bread and inhaled the fruits and vegetables as if he'd hardly eaten anything in an entire week.

The stiffness in his injured arm bothered him, and he dared to untie the sling from his shoulder and stretch his joints out onto his lap. His sore, aching muscles cried out in protest, but otherwise, the stretching relieved much of the tightness running rampant through his elbow.

Next, he carefully unwrapped the damp bandage from around his head, hissing when his fingers accidentally brushed against the injury. However, after a week of healing, it hurt far less than it had when he'd first woken from the fiery pain.

Thankfully, the bandage was clean, which meant the bleeding had stopped.

He decided to check on the wound on his side later when he didn't have an audience witnessing him lifting his shirt. Slowly, he stood, careful with his movements to keep himself from blacking out or toppling over.

"Will one of you lovely young ladies escort me outside? I could use a breath of fresh air."

Senna and Lily jumped to their feet, each grasping onto one of his elbows before he had a chance to blink in surprise. Like an old man struggling to walk without his cane, they helped him hobble outside.

And the moment the sunshine hit his face, he breathed in deeply and basked in the warmth.

But then an overwhelming hopelessness crashed over his head when he faced the sprawling green fields of an unfamiliar territory. The land stretched up and over a hill to one side, and the other led to a road to who knew where. He spotted a small orchard, a garden teeming with produce, and a barn.

He had absolutely no idea where he was.

And the thought terrified him.

Chapter Four

"Don't overexert yourself," Ivette warned.

Ben grunted in response as he dragged a large branch off to the side and stacked it next to a bundle of other branches leaning against a tree. His head spun with the physical effort, and his side protested as the movement pulled on his wound.

But he refused to leave these five women to fend for themselves after the recent storm had dislodged branches from trees and scattered them across the fields.

Breathing heavily, he placed his hands on his hips to survey the remainder of the mess. Small branches remained, but they'd cleared most of the larger ones.

Helen giggled as she threw a stick, only for one of the neighbor's dogs to race after it excitedly and return it moments later, panting for more. Grace wandered off on her own, clearing the debris in the farther fields. Senna and Lily remained close, each demanding his attention and talking his ear off.

And Ivette...

She kept insisting he sit down rather than help with the chores. But it didn't sit right with him to stand around while others worked.

"I'm doing fine," he said after catching his breath, casting a smile in her direction. He enjoyed the way her face colored, and he couldn't help himself as he admired her. Her copper hair reached her lower waist like a molten waterfall, and he couldn't deny how he enjoyed that she didn't wear her hair back often, but rather let the long strands hang loose around her shoulders.

The freckles on her face endeared him to her even more, giving her a uniquely beautiful quality about her he knew he wasn't used to seeing wherever he was from.

He cleared his throat and glanced away when he realized he was staring. But to his credit, she had been staring right back.

Of course, all the older Danvers sisters were beautiful in their own unique way. But there was something about Ivette... Her selfless drive to do what must be done was attractive.

Not that he was noticing...

"Ben!" Lily called, interrupting the small moment with Ivette. She latched onto his arm and steered him in the opposite direction. "I'm sure you're hungry. I made you a snack inside."

"Oh." He politely squeezed her fingers and pulled her hand from his arm. "A snack sounds wonderful. I'll be inside after I bathe."

True, his clothes clung to his sweaty body, and he worried he stank like the animals he shared a barn with at night these past couple of days. But in reality, he needed…quiet. A place to go to be vulnerable as he fought off the pain and the sickness and the dizziness without witnesses.

He should have listened to Ivette. His body wasn't ready for this.

"It will be waiting!" she sang cheerfully as she took Senna's arm instead, and they giggled and whispered to one another as they made their way toward the house.

He tapped down his nausea to the best of his ability as he slowly made his way toward the edge of the trees. Only when the shadows of the boughs overhead shaded him from view did he instinctively clutch his side. He hissed when touching the wound still pained him, even after over a week since the accident.

His head spun. His stomach clenched. And unable to hold back any longer, he stumbled toward a bush and retched.

And retched some more.

Until his stomach emptied itself of what he ate earlier that morning and continued to empty until he tasted foul bile in his mouth.

He slumped exhaustedly against the trunk of a tree near the small brook, sitting with one leg propped up and the other outstretched in front of him. He leaned his head back against the smooth bark, taking deep breaths to calm the agony in his side, his head, and his stomach.

A twig snapped to the left of him, and he jumped at the sound but winced when the movement pulled on his side wound. His heart picked up its rhythm when Ivette's hazel gaze honed in on him. She didn't stop beside him, but rather continued toward the stream.

"I'm supposed to be bathing," he chuckled weakly as his head rolled in her direction. "What will your sisters think?"

"Oh, hush." She dipped a handkerchief into the stream, wrung it out, and placed the damp cloth over his forehead. The coolness helped relieve some of the ache festering at his temples. "They will simply bemoan at a missed-out opportunity."

Her face reddened not for the first time that day, and he couldn't help but laugh at her flirtatious wit. At least until his side seized and his laugh turned into a cry of pain.

"Let me see," she demanded.

He struggled to lift his shirt, so she did it for him. And frowned when the fabric was spotted with blood. "You really must let this heal, Ben. Gallivanting around the fields is not helping you."

"I hate sitting around and doing nothing."

"All I'm trying to suggest..." She bit her tongue in an adorable manner as she turned his head to the side to inspect his injury. "...unless you allow yourself to heal, you will only make this worse for yourself."

He offered an easy grin to try to belie his flaring pain. "You sound like quite the doctor."

However, she didn't return his smile. Her mouth turned into a melancholy frown as she sat back on her heels and stared at her knees. "This is not the first time I've had to doctor someone on the brink of death."

She didn't elaborate, and he didn't want to press her for more information. "I'm not sure I properly thanked you for..." He gestured with his good arm toward the cliffside peeking out between a cluster of trees. "I've never met anyone like you, Ivette."

Laughter escaped her as she shook her head and gave him a pointed look. "How in the nine kingdoms could you possibly know that?"

He joined in with his own laughter and shrugged one shoulder. "I suppose I can't say for certain. But nevertheless, I feel confident in my statement."

He watched as she averted her gaze and trailed her hair through her fingers. Her mouth opened and closed as if she tried to come up with a response to his compliment.

When she still didn't speak, he bit his lip and tentatively asked, "Can you… erm… help me with… erm…" He gestured to his shirt. One of his arms worked fine. The other? It still hurt to bend. "I really do mean to bathe. I smell like vomit and cow dung."

"A-a-ah, y-y-yes. Of c-c-course."

Ivette unfastened the top button of his shirt and worked her way down, and when she lifted her head and met his watchful gaze, his stomach flipped, and his heart raced. Heat climbed his neck at the way her fingers brushed against his skin, at how her flustered gaze held steady, creating a pleasant tension between them.

A desire for her stirred warmth in his belly, and he wanted to pull her closer, to bridge the gap between them and kiss her.

But he forced his hands to remain at his sides while she finished unbuttoning his shirt and helped him to his feet. Her strength surprised him, attesting to her time spent doing manual chores on the farm.

A part of him liked that she wasn't a fragile little woman. She was tall, yet still a head shorter than him. She was slender but strong, exuding confidence in every one of her movements. At the same time, she still managed to appear graceful and feminine.

He blinked several times to break him out of his fixation on her. He needed to focus on himself and getting home. Not on a pretty face and a breathtaking smile.

By the heavens, it was difficult.

"Do you need help with…" With a nod of her head, she gestured to his shirt.

"I think I've got it."

Awkwardly, he tried to twist his good arm out of his sleeve. But the movement spun his surroundings until he tipped precariously to the side. He tried to right himself but overcorrected and stumbled forward. The toe of his boot caught against a protruding root and sent him sprawling toward the stream.

"Gah!" he cried, unable to catch himself as he splashed into the frigid, shallow water, just deep enough to take part of the blow to prevent the fall from paining him.

"Ben!" Ivette gasped.

Like him, she didn't seem to spot the root he'd tripped on. He tried to call out a warning, but then she, too, released a startled yelp as her shoe caught as well. She shrieked moments before she landed on top of him, water splashing around them.

He caught her with his good arm, but her weight landing on him still managed to pain his side. Still, he tried not to show it.

Frigid water washed over them and soaked into their hair and clothing. For a moment, they were a tangle of fabric and limbs and branches. At least before Ivette gasped and lifted her head.

"I apologize!" she said, struggling to free herself and her sodden skirts from him. When she attempted to lift herself off him, the skirts must have dragged her back down, because she crashed onto him again.

"Oof!" he grunted.

"I'm so sorry." She lifted much of her weight off him once again, and for a moment, they held each other's gaze. But then her nose wrinkled in a teasing manner. "You really *do* smell like vomit and cow dung."

He couldn't help himself as he cracked a smile, his amusement over the situation turning into laughter. He splashed water into her face, and she shrieked before retaliating until they were both laughing.

Finally, Ivette managed to free herself and helped him out of his shirt and shoes but no more. He grinned as he watched her retreating back and the way the bottom half of her wetted hair swung with each of her steps.

"You don't want to miss out on the *opportunity*, do you?" he called after her, repeating her earlier words. He laughed when she glanced over her shoulder, and her blush made its entrance right on time before she rolled her eyes and continued on her way.

He forced his gaze away and frowned. Flirting was not going to get him home. Despite knowing that, the only image he could recall when thinking about home was a beautiful set of hazel eyes, sprawling green fields filled with sheep, and endless blue skies.

What if he never recovered his memories?

It won't be so bad, he reassured himself. Because he was content with the new home he'd found. But despite Ivette insisting he needed to rest, he wanted to earn his place.

No matter how much time he might spend here.

Chapter Five

Apparently, nothing motivated women more than having a handsome man in the house.

Ivette was shocked when Lily willingly volunteered to do more housework, when Senna weeded the garden without being asked, when Grace finished milking the cow before sunrise. Of course, Helen shirked more of her chores to regale Ben with story after story, talking nearly nonstop while following the poor man around.

But he took it in stride with kindness and patience, and he even rewarded her with smiles or laughter.

Ivette had insisted he stay until he either regained his memories or someone he knew came to find him. On the one hand, his presence was a great motivator. On the other…she feared he would break a few hearts too many when he eventually left.

Not including her own, of course.

A huff of exertion left her lips as she hitched the horse to the wagon, and not for the first time, she cursed her father for leaving them to fend for themselves. What she wouldn't do for a set of strong muscles around the house.

She froze before rolling her eyes at her stupidity. She *did* have a strapping pair of muscles eager to help around the homestead. Although she didn't want Ben to overexert himself until he healed a bit more, perhaps there were a few things she could ask him to do while she had him.

A pit of guilt wormed its way into her stomach when she admitted only to herself why she was unwilling to part with him. If he had money to spare, she could desperately use some of it. But he couldn't part with something he didn't remember having.

Senna loaded several bags of wool into the back of the wagon to sell in town, along with a variety of squash and melons to trade. "Where's Ben?" she asked.

Frowning, Ivette finished bridling the horse. "I thought he was with you."

"He said he was going to fix the fence on the hill," Helen volunteered in a sing-song voice before she boarded the wagon.

Her eyes flew open wide as she snapped her head in the direction of the hill. "No! He can't be up there!"

She picked up her skirts and left her sisters with the wagon as she sprinted toward the hill. Her gaze frantically darted about in search of him, lingering especially on the steep drop to the ground below. When she didn't find his body there, she climbed the hill.

Only for her heart to settle with relief when she found him wrestling with several wooden planks, a hammer, and nails.

He grimaced when he glanced at her, and not for the first time—and certainly not the last—his blue eyes sparked heat inside her chest. The heat traveled down to her stomach, and then her toes, until she breathed heavily over something other than the exertion of climbing the hill.

"I learned the hard way that my past self is not quite as handy as I hoped to be." He held up a bent nail and a red, inflamed finger and winced apologetically. "I am useless with a hammer. But I can't just leave the fence like this. One of the sheep might fall."

She placed a steadying hand over her heart, but it did nothing to slow the rapid beat from her lingering fear and fluster.

Finally, she managed to speak. "You will want to discard the broken pieces entirely and start with a new crossbeam." She reached for one of the planks of wood. "But set it on *this* side of the poles. It's safer in case something was to lean against the fence." She grimaced when she realized what she'd said. "Well, I did say saf*er*, not completely safe."

They reached for a nail at the same time, and when their fingers brushed, the rush of heat from the contact moved up her hand, her arms, and straight into her cheeks. The heat only worsened when they met each other's gaze.

His mouth twitched on one side, the simple sight fixing her to the spot as if she were a tree catching feelings—no, err, roots.

The tip of his finger brushed her knuckle, almost imperceptibly, but enough for her to feel it.

"You know…" Another caress of his finger. "Your freckles are uniquely beautiful."

She quickly snatched her hand back and glared at him, effectively breaking the spell he held over her. No one had ever told her that her freckles were beautiful. Rather, she was teased relentlessly growing up over her copper hair and noticeable freckles others called blemishes.

"Let's finish this fence quickly," she said in a curt tone, averting her gaze from his captivating stare. "We're headed into town soon, and I would like you to accompany us if you are able." She held one of the planks while he hammered it in, this time without smashing his finger. "It's a good starting point for finding your kin."

"We should probably face it," he grunted as he held the next beam, his body clearly still straining against his injuries, while she hammered. "No one's coming for me. It's been two weeks already. Perhaps I don't have a family."

She shook her head and looked him up and down. He wore his vest today, looking like the ever impeccably dressed rich man stranded on a farm. "You look too important to be forgotten. Someone will come. I'm sure of it."

He snorted at her comment but otherwise said nothing more as they finished repairing the broken fence. Only when Ben picked up the remaining bucket of nails and hammer did he comment.

"Are you sure there was nothing else on my person to help identify me?" he asked, his forehead creased with concern. "A letter? A weapon? A ring?"

She glanced at his bare fingers, unease punching her in the gut, surprising her that she'd feel it at all. "Would you have had a ring on you? Are you married?"

"No." He shook his head. "I'm certain I'm not. But…" He lifted his hand closer to her face and pointed out the imprint of where a ring must have lain recently on his pinky finger, as if he'd worn it all day, every day. "Perhaps I got robbed."

"You wouldn't have your pocket watch if that were the case. *And…*" She led them around the sheep grazing in the lower field. One lifted its head and bleated at them. "You did have your horse last I saw you. Best case scenario, your horse will return home, and when someone finds it without a rider, if they haven't already, they will send an entire search party."

If only the horse had left visible tracks, then they might have been able to track it down. But the rain had washed away any evidence of its existence entirely.

"We'll figure this out." She placed a comforting hand on his arm but quickly snatched it back as if he'd burned her and hurried toward the wagon. The sooner the man left, the better.

Because she refused to allow hers to be one of the hearts he shattered when he was gone.

The rickety wagon did nothing to soothe the lingering aches of Ben's injuries, rocking back and forth, back and forth, and lurching uncomfortably when a wheel rolled over a rock in the road.

He closed his eyes to ward off the ache but quickly thought better of it when his stomach rolled with queasiness.

"Well, aren't you having a hard time of it," Ivette commented from where she sat up front on the driver's bench with Helen beside her. She held the reins in a firm grip and kept her gaze forward, but clearly, she spoke to him.

Ben brushed a piece of straw off his lap and rested his head against the side of the rumbling wagon. "I have no idea what you're talking about," he quipped. "I have not retched once."

Senna and Lily giggled across from him, and Ivette revealed the faintest smile as she kept her attention forward.

He took a moment to study her. She sat straight in the seat, appearing relaxed. But he noticed the rigidness of her shoulders, the set of her jaw, the white-knuckled grip of her fingers over the reins.

She was afraid. But why?

Another conundrum came to mind as he placed his arms behind his head to help absorb some of the jarring movement of the wagon. When were the girls' parents coming home?

He assumed they left Avorstead for something like taxes or business. But he didn't know how to ask such a simple question. None of them spoke about their parents. And he wondered if he shouldn't either.

The town was still a decent way down the road, so he filled the silence. Because he decided he didn't like the silence. It was too…uncomfortable. If there was too much silence, then he had no choice but to dwell on…on what?

He batted away the frustration with a smile as he pulled his attention to the other three women across from him. "What do you like to do in your spare time?"

Senna answered first. "Making clothes. Shirts and dresses and hats. Someday, I hope to find a seamstress job in the big city."

Despite the peasant clothing she wore, he noticed she was dressed nicely with a straw hat on her head with a long, blue bow tied over it. The blues and greens of her dress flattered her complexion and the blonde of her hair.

"Painting," Lily answered next with a shy smile. "When we have supplies. I mostly draw with charcoal."

Grace didn't answer, but rather held a book to her chest and stared out over the fields passing behind them. But Helen turned around in her seat with excited, lively eyes.

"Ivette taught me how to read, but I'm still not really good at it. I love when she reads me stories or makes them up from her head! She tells me a story every night before bed. Ever since I was…" The girl counted on her fingers with her tongue wedged between her teeth. "Ever since I was five!"

The color of Ivette's knuckles grew whiter at the mention, and he couldn't help but inhale sharply as he finally came to the realization.

Their parents were gone. And Ivette took care of them. All of them.

No wonder she appeared so tired. No wonder she fretted over them and saw to many of their basic needs. Of course, the others helped with chores, but he noticed Ivette taking on the hardest of the work. She cooked the meals. She fixed the things that broke. She saw to their well-being. And his.

And she did it all without complaint.

His expression softened as his gaze shifted from Ivette and back to Helen. "I'm sure she tells the best stories. I, for one, would love to hear a tale."

"They are fairy tales," Ivette said with a pinched expression. "Surely, you would have no interest in such fables."

"Then you need to get to know me better."

"I think you need to get to know yourself better first."

He burst into laughter at her quick wit, which brought out an endearing flush to her face. She sure was beautiful when she blushed.

But then he quickly sobered when the aching pit in his chest surfaced and swelled until he could hardly draw breath. He didn't understand why he felt this way in Ivette's presence. And a part of him didn't want to know.

Finally, the wagon lurched into town, joining with other wagons, horses, carts, and people on the road. They passed houses and businesses, horses and oxen.

Ben watched the people in fascination as they called out a greeting to the Danvers sisters, and many of them cast him curious—and even suspicious—glances. With a wave and a smile, the suspicion melted in favor of intrigue or flustered smiles. He winked at one of the women standing beside a horse, and her face lit up in a blush, a hand flying to rest over her heart.

The wagon rolled to a stop off to the side of the road in a patch of empty field next to other carts and wagons. He pushed through the unsteadiness of his feet and grabbed a bag of wool before climbing down from the wagon. But just as his feet touched the ground, Ivette snatched the bag from him and stomped away, leaving him staring with confusion at her retreating back.

A heavy ache sat on his chest as he watched her go.

"Why do you dislike me?" he whispered to himself.

He recalled the curt words she often gave him, the glares, and now this. Did she feel burdened by his presence at their home? Had he disrupted the peace in their lives by his abrupt arrival?

He turned back to the wagon and grabbed the remaining two bags of wool and followed. She didn't even glance his way as he set the bags on a countertop of a booth in the crowded market square. She haggled with the shop owner to get a good price for the wool, but the man kept shaking his head and going lower and lower until the offers were ridiculously unfair.

Although he didn't know how much a regular bag of wool was worth, what he *did* know was men often looked down on women just because they were *women*. As if they were dumb and uneducated and worthless because of what they were born with. Or lack thereof.

"Excuse me," Ben said, interrupting the haggling to reach out his hand. "Ben Harding. I didn't catch your name."

The man abandoned Ivette entirely to shake his hand. "Ivan Storres. I run the fabric shop with my wife, Gertrude."

"I can see that." Ben picked up one of the balls of yarn in a basket and inspected the soft quality and the vibrant colors. "Beautiful work. Do you dye these yourselves?"

Ivan puffed out his chest proudly and nodded. "You won't find quality like this anywhere else."

"Who is your supplier?"

"Ah. Well." The man cleared his throat and fiddled with a stack of yarn before he gestured to Ivette still standing forgotten beside the booth.

Ben cast a disarming smile at the man as he returned the yarn. "The quality of the wool is unmatched. You are lucky you have such a wonderful supplier." He patted the booth.

"I'll be sure to send customers your way. It was a pleasure to meet you, Ivan."

As he walked away, he heard Ivan grumbling under his breath before the clinking of coins reached his ears. Moments later, footsteps crunching over rocks and dirt alerted him to Ivette's approach. But when he turned, he flinched at the thunderous look on her face.

"I don't need your help," she hissed, her eyes carrying a suspicious sheen in them. "I've done this by myself for six years, and I don't need anyone's help now."

Before he managed to utter a word, she stomped away into the crowd with her sisters.

And he couldn't help but stare after her until her long, copper hair disappeared from view.

"Ah! There he is!" Someone released a loud, hearty chuckle, and instinctually, Ben adopted an easy smile as he faced a burly man with tattoos stretched across his arms. "The man who survived a broken neck and a shattered skull."

Ben laughed and socked him playfully in the shoulder. "I think you have the tale mixed up. Who are you, anyway?"

"The name's Vincent Keswick. I came by every day to help your lazy, unconscious arse with the dressing and other…*things*."

The knowledge should have mortified him, but he could only release a relieved whoosh of breath. "Thank the fires of oblivion. I thought Ivette might have seen something she probably shouldn't have."

When Vincent didn't answer, he turned to find a smirk growing across the man's face. "Ivette, huh? There are three, nearly four, eligible women to choose from in that household, and you're falling for *her*."

With an accompanying scoff, he rolled his eyes and punched his new friend, but harder this time. "I'm not falling for anyone. She's the one who saved me, the one who took the brunt of my caretaking."

"*But* you have to admit she's pretty, eh?"

Ben scoffed again, but rather than denying it, he searched for her and found the sheen of copper beneath the afternoon sun. His gaze trailed her movements across the town square. She held herself with confidence. She was so sure of herself, her feet planted on solid ground rather than floating somewhere in the clouds. She was like a rock. Sturdy. Immovable. Crushing anything in its path. Yet, she exuded grace and femininity, beautiful in every sense of the word.

But whenever he looked at her… Shame crept up into his chest and made a permanent nest, and he couldn't help but glance away.

Like now, as he lowered his gaze to his feet and frowned.

What had he done in his past to warrant such shame? He truly didn't want to give into the fear that perhaps…that perhaps he wasn't a good man. Because he wanted to be a good man. He wanted to reflect Ivette's breathtaking light like the moon glowing in the night sky in conjunction with the sun. But he worried he didn't deserve it.

"You know…" Vincent said slowly, breaking him out of his thoughts as he stroked the facial hair on his chin. "You speak like someone who hails from Edilann."

He wrinkled his nose as he tried to recall the name in his mind, only to come up blank. "Where is that?"

The man crossed his arms and nodded his head toward the east. "It's the next kingdom over. You've come a long way from home if you're from there."

"How far is it?"

"A couple days by wagon to reach the border. Another two to reach the city."

"Huh." He lifted his head to watch the Danvers women ogle the hats and ribbons at a booth. In the small amount of time he'd known them, they'd weaseled their way into his heart. Leaving Avorstead was not something he wanted to do, but it was something he needed to do. Somewhere out there, he was *somebody*. And he needed to find out who.

As soon as riding in a bumpy wagon for more than a few minutes wouldn't threaten to crack his skull open. He had a while yet before he was fit for traveling.

But after the incident with Ivette, he feared he'd overstayed his welcome.

He shuffled his feet as he tore his gaze away, finding it difficult to do so. "Do you know if there is any work for me in town?"

Vincent raised an eyebrow as he looked him up and down. "You're closer to toppling over than doing any sort of work with your head on straight." He shrugged and stroked his beard. "What are you good at?"

A huff left Ben's lips. "I don't know."

"Well…" He nodded his head toward the market booths. "Go on and find out. Surely, something must catch your eye, eh?"

With a nod, Ben stepped out from the safety of his little corner and perused the market square. Yarn. Ribbons. Fabric. Clothing. Food. Livestock. He spotted a section of the market teeming with children, many begging their parents for coins to spend playing games and winning prizes.

He watched the children with a smile growing across his face. Some battled each other by wrestling a stick away from the other. First to lose their footing lost. Other adults played gambling games with dice, or men wrestling pigs.

He froze in front of a booth filled with all kinds of liquor from blackberry wine to mulberry gin to honey mead. His throat dried, suddenly parched as he stared at the variety of bottles with longing. Perspiration dotted his hands and brow. His heart quickened. His neck heated. And he found himself wanting a sip more than he'd wanted anything since he'd woken from his injuries.

No!

His mind screamed the word so loudly as to startle him backward, away from the booth he hadn't realized he'd approached.

Ducking his head, he hurried away from the booth and the temptation it offered, all while shame pricked at the back of his neck. Not just because he'd wanted a drink. But because he realized *why* he likely felt shame around Ivette.

There was no doubt about it. In the past, he was a drunkard. And consuming alcohol often led to other things. Things he likely wasn't proud of.

Things Ivette would hate him for.

Ivette…

It was always Ivette. He was not falling for her. He *wasn't*.

But her opinion of him mattered to him.

It's too late, his mind whispered to the all-consuming shame. *What's done is done. You can't take it back.*

Take *what* back?

He wanted to scream at the skies, at fate for stealing his memories and filling his head with air. These things he could only speculate, and he wanted to know if they were true.

A *whistle clatter* pulled him out of his screaming, frustrated thoughts and toward a knife-throwing game on the opposite side of the road. Several people gathered around a young man, who threw a knife toward a wall of wood with strategically placed apples dangling from twine at different levels.

The knife hit the board by the hilt and clattered to the ground like the previous one.

The game owner hissed through his teeth and collected the fallen knives. "Better luck next time, lad."

Ben approached the booth, feeling many pairs of eyes on him as he surveyed the five knives the man placed in a neat row on the wooden booth.

"Wanna try your luck?" The man grinned, revealing a couple missing teeth and one with a rotten black tint.

He shrugged regretfully. "I don't have any mon—"

Someone reached past him and placed a coin on the counter, and he inhaled his surprise when he found Ivette beside him. She glanced up at him with an apologetic expression, as if trying to make up for the outburst earlier.

"What's the prize?" he asked, never taking his gaze off her. Her green-gold eyes were beautiful. Captivating. And the mere sight of them twisted his insides until they stole the breath from him completely.

The man shook a pouch of coins, pulling his attention back to the booth. "Each coin spent to play gets placed into the purse. If someone manages to hit all five apples in one game out of eight tries, they get the entire pool of coin. If no one manages it…" He laughed and threw the bag into the air before catching it with a jangle of coins. "Then I get to keep it. So far, no one has managed to strike all five."

He didn't know how much coin lay inside, but he knew it was enough to get him to Edilann.

Laughing, the booth keeper instructed him to stand beside the stall and throw the knives from there.

Ben picked up one of the knives from the counter and inspected his target. The faint breeze jostled the apples the slightest bit, the dangling fruit more slippery at the edge of a knife than one that was stationary.

He'd need to hit the target directly in the center for the best chance to embed the sharp tips into the juicy flesh.

He raised his arm, and the audience hushed as if collectively holding their breath. And then with a flick of his wrist, he sent the knife flying toward the target. The tip of the knife impaled the fruit and stuck fast into the wood on the other side.

Ben reeled back in shock, as he'd fully expected to miss.

Applause and shouts of excitement rippled around him, but he only managed to stare at the juice dripping from the fruit. Beginner's luck, surely.

The handle of the next knife fit nicely in his hand as he hesitantly picked it up, noting that the tip was slightly bent from others who had used the knife before him. He eyed the top right apple dangling from a shorter string, and once again, the audience hushed.

It was almost comical the way silence ensued. But it *did* help his concentration as he threw the second knife. It, too, struck the apple. Instead of embedding in the wood behind it, it now dangled along with the fruit.

"Oh!" He laughed as he turned to face his enthusiastic audience. "I'm actually good at this!"

He picked up the third knife with more confidence in his movement and his grip, noticing how the crowd had tripled around him. He tossed the knife, and sure enough, it struck its target.

The crowd cheered wildly. He pumped his fist. Two more knives remained. But what didn't remain was the booth keeper's toothless grin.

He caught Ivette's eye, noticing the surprised part of her lips, her wide eyes taken aback. She didn't cheer for him like her sisters but rather offered a quiet confidence.

Taking a deep breath, he turned and let loose the fourth knife. Sure enough, it pierced the target barely through the side rather than the middle.

As he reached for the fifth knife, the booth keeper snatched it away and replaced it with another one. "The tip was bent," he explained with a devious glint in his eye. "This one is far sturdier."

However, as he handled the small weapon, he noticed the knife felt largely off center and imbalanced. He didn't want to call the man out on it, and instead adjusted his grip.

"This one's for you, Ivette Danvers." He winked at her and kissed the flat edge of the knife, enjoying the way her entire face lit up with a furious blush.

He faced the target, and with the flick of his wrist, the knife soared through the air and speared the remaining apple straight through its heart.

The crowd roared wildly. People jostled him and slapped him congratulatory on the back. And though he didn't quite enjoy getting tossed around when his injuries still hurt, he couldn't find it in himself to frown when the booth keeper reluctantly handed the coin pouch over with a glare.

He held up the pouch triumphantly, which received another wave of shouting and cheering. He laughed at the enthusiasm because it was only a simple game. But he highly suspected no one had managed to beat it before.

Surprisingly, a lot more coin lay within the pouch than he realized, and he used some of it to buy himself a shaving kit, as he preferred himself clean shaven. He bought a dragon figurine crafted of weaved grass for Helen, a book for Grace, ribbons for Senna, and paint for Lily. For Ivette, he perused the stalls a bit longer, trying to find something she might like. She was more practical than the others, so when he found a knife-sharpening block small enough to tuck away into the kitchen, he didn't hesitate to trade it for coin.

His gifts for the girls tucked into a satchel, he located them beside the wagon, waiting on Ivette to return with the remainder of the supplies they needed. And when she did, she appeared tired enough to fall asleep on her feet.

He took the supplies from her, and this time it went without a glare or complaint. In fact, she didn't look at him at all, even as everyone clambered into the back, and she urged the horse forward by the reins.

Ivette's shoulders slumped with pure exhaustion. Her hair lay in an adorable mess as if it had tangled during her quest for supplies. But dark circles lay beneath her eyes, attesting to her lack of sleep over the past…who knew how long?

The other sisters talked animatedly to one another, not sharing their sister's exhaustion in the slightest.

He smiled when Senna's conversation turned to him and the knife-throwing game. But it was hard to keep his gaze from slipping from Ivette.

He wanted to ease her burdens. He only wished he knew how.

Chapter Six

"How could he do this!" Senna stormed into the house with a handful of ribbons and a crinkled letter fisted in her palm. Tears trailed down her face, emotion blotching red across her cheeks. "He didn't even say goodbye. He only left a lousy note."

The breath faltered from Ivette's lungs. Blood rushed through her ears. She stared at the wall behind Senna's shoulder, the rest of her sister's words drowning in the frozen disbelief washing through her veins. Panic clutched at her racing heart, and her floury hands gripped the edge of the counter as her legs suddenly decided they would rather collapse than hold her upright.

Ben was gone? And he gave Senna a letter but not her?

"This is your fault!" Senna cried. "If you'd only been nicer to him, perhaps he might have wanted to stay!"

"My fault?" Fury boiled through her blood, and she took a moment to breathe deeply to allow herself to reply in a calm manner like her mother had taught her so many years ago. "You and Lily cling to him every chance you get, never giving him room to breathe, and you think it's my fault?"

Senna swiped the tears from her face. As if her even reply helped soothe her emotions, Senna also responded calmly. "I suppose we have been a little bit much. But he treats us like ladies, unlike the swine living in town."

Ivette snorted and returned to her task of kneading dough for the bread they were to eat for supper. The familiar stretch and fold, stretch and fold pounded in conjunction with the ache throbbing in her chest.

"Those young men need to grow up if they want a chance with you."

Stretch and fold. Stretch and fold.

She sniffed back the tears forming in her own eyes.

"I told you I'm going to focus on my career as a seamstress in the city," Senna said in a haughty tone. "I refuse to settle down here. Even if some faces are rather tempting."

The door hinge creaked open and shut as one of her sisters entered the cottage. She tsked and hid her crumbling heart with flour and kneading and an air of nonchalance. "That man is handsome, and he knows it. That's all I have to say—"

"Why, thank you."

She gasped and spun around, only for her eyes to fly open when she found the man in question standing in her kitchen, his blue eyes blazing with amusement. "Ben!"

He grinned and leaned a shoulder against the wall, gesturing to her. "Go on. I'd like to hear what you have to say."

Wide-eyed Senna slipped conveniently outside, leaving Ivette floundering on her own.

But her mouth opened and closed as fluster claimed every inch of her face and tied her tongue into knots. Finally, words stumbled out of her mouth. "I-I-I thought you l-l-left."

"Not yet." His grin widened, and he stared at her like a wolf ready to pounce on a sheep. "I tried to find Helen to say goodbye, but I haven't managed to track her down. And, of course, I was saving the best for last."

"Stop it." She pulled off a piece of her dough and lobbed it at him. His reflexes were too slow to dodge, and it hit him on the chest before flopping onto the floor. "You flirt with anything that gives you doe eyes and wears a skirt. I meant what I said."

She turned her back to him but acutely felt his stare and his presence in the small room. Her heart picked up its pace as his footsteps neared, and the heat from his body seared into her back.

Just ignore him, and he'll go away.

But it was impossible to ignore him when his welcome heat seeped into the small space between them, when his warm exhale caressed her ear, when his finger brushed against her cheek to remove the flour from her skin.

She couldn't help herself as she leaned back, desperate for the heat he offered and whatever else he might give. Her will to fight him sank below shaky waters the moment his hand rested over her arm and traveled down the length to her elbow, and then to her wrist. Her hand…

And then her will shattered entirely as he trailed his fingers over hers where they rested on the flour-coated counter.

"Well, there is a certain woman who *doesn't* seem to know how beautiful she is," he murmured in her ear. "And I think she should know it more often."

A shaky breath escaped her lungs at his lingering touch, and her eyelids fluttered closed when his smooth cheek rested against hers.

He set something on the counter and released her, effectively pulling her out of the trance he put her in like a deer hypnotized by a carriage approaching quickly down the road.

Her eyebrows drew together when she spotted a knife-sharpening block, a coin purse, and a folded paper resting on top. She picked up the note and turned around.

Only to realize Ben was gone, as if he'd only been a figment of her imagination.

However, the flour prints on top of her fingers proved he was real, that he'd touched her in such a sweet, intimate manner.

Confusion still lingering on her brow, she unfolded the parchment and read the neat scrawl across the page.

Dearest Ivette,

I can't thank you enough for all you've done for me. You saved my life. I will never forget that. My offerings for compensation are meager in comparison, but I wanted to give back in some way. Careful. Your knives are now sharp.

Vincent said I might come from Edilann, so I'm headed there. Perhaps someone might recognize me.

I apologize for being a burden. I know I'm quite useless in many areas on the farm, and lying about retching my guts out didn't help much either. You are wonderful. You are an incredible big sister, and I know they all look up to you.

Perhaps our paths might cross again.
All my adoration,
Ben (?)

Her hand flew to her mouth as her gaze darted to the window in an attempt to catch a glimpse of him. He truly was leaving. Because of her being short with him at the market? Or because he truly wanted to find his identity even when he was not yet fit for travel?

Ivette scrambled for one of the knives in the block, pulled it out, and cut a perfect slice down the middle of her dough loaf, meeting no resistance from a dull blade.

Ben had not only noticed her knives were dull, but he'd gone through the lengths of sharpening them for her.

Next, she opened the coin pouch and realized much of what lay inside was his earnings from winning the knife-throwing game. Emotion clogged her throat. At his kindness. At his selflessness.

The thought of him leaving created a hole inside her heart.

"Ben!" she gasped, lifting her skirts as she scrambled after him. "Ben, wait!"

She threw the door open but froze when a chill of dread passed over her, similar to what she had felt moments before Ben had fallen from the cliffside.

Beneath a dark, cloudy sky, three masked men thundered through the fields on horseback with ropes in their hands. One of the rustlers lassoed their rope around the neck of a large sheep. The livestock started to panic, and only then did she notice the hound snapping at their legs as it tried to corner them.

The sheep bleated and began to stampede through the field.

"Stop!" Ivette screamed.

Losing even one of their sheep could be catastrophic. But all of them? She snatched a shovel resting against the side of the house and didn't hesitate as she rushed toward them.

But then a small scream turned her blood to ice. Standing in the middle of the stampede, the sheep only narrowly avoiding her…

"Helen!"

Ivette was too far away to help Helen. And Ben was without a large weapon, as he only possessed a small knife tucked in his boot.

He stooped down to pick up a handful of fist-sized rocks and lobbed them toward the rustlers. One hit a man in the shoulder. Another struck his jaw. The third rock smashed into the man's throat, and he turned his mount and fled while choking against the hit.

Ben moved closer and threw several more stones. The first missed. The second hit the man's leg. The third crashed into his nose with a sickening *crack*.

Helen screamed as she lost her footing and fell backward, getting lost entirely in the stampeding sheep.

The third rustler forgotten, Ben sprinted to where he last saw the girl. Without a thought for himself, he threw himself into the stampede.

The sheep knocked him one way and then the other. Bleats and pounding hooves nearly blinded his senses with their deafening blare. He barely managed to keep himself from falling to his knees as the sheep jostled him.

"Helen!" he shouted. "Helen!"

When she didn't answer, he pushed himself farther into the stampede. But a rather large sheep crashed into him, sending him sprawling onto the grass.

Sheep leaped over him. Some parted for him. Others shoved him to the side.

But he kept crawling forward, searching for the girl while trying to protect his head from further injury.

His heart soared when he spotted the flowery pattern of her dress through the chaos of black and white. He crawled toward her, hissing as several sheep used him as a stool, their heavy weight pressing into his back.

Finally, he latched onto Helen's foot and pulled her toward him and into the safety of his arms. It took all his effort to push himself to his knees and then his feet. The sheep jostled him again, but he kept a firm hold on Helen's limp body.

He swallowed back his fear when he glanced down and found blood smeared across her cheek, dripping from her temple.

Gritting his teeth, he fought his way across the river of frantic sheep until he stumbled out of the herd and onto green grass.

"Yah!" the remaining rustler shouted, and he spared a glance behind him to find the masked man leading two sheep away with a rope around their necks. But the man stopped just long enough to pull down the handkerchief to stare at Ben, and he stared back.

Something about the man's face… He'd seen it before. But where?

Who are you? he mouthed.

The man's brows furrowed, but then his gaze snapped to Ivette, who still moved toward them holding a shovel. The rustler kicked his horse's flanks and disappeared in the opposite direction.

With his hands full, Ben couldn't pursue the man and the stolen livestock. Instead, he hurried toward Ivette, who rushed toward them with terror in her eyes.

"Mercy!" she gasped, breathing heavily as she threw down her shovel and smoothed down the girl's sticky hair. "No, no, no. Not again. Not again. Please, no!"

"She'll need stitches."

Ivette's frantic gaze searched behind her until it fell on her sisters, each frozen to the spot. "Senna!" she cried, and he followed as she approached the house. "Stitches. Please."

Senna's face paled as she glanced at Helen, and although she said nothing, she nodded and ducked inside.

Ben paused to check for a pulse, and thankfully he found Helen's heart beating wildly at her neck. Blood still rushed down her cheek, as one of the sheep's hooves must have caught her on the temple hard enough to knock her out. He desperately hoped there was no more damage than that.

Grace held the door open for him as he followed Ivette down the short hallway and into one of the two rooms on the right. Three beds were tucked against the walls, creating very little space to move about.

He set the girl down on the bed with a corn-husk doll on the pillow, and Ivette stepped in to press a cloth to her head while Senna readied the needle and thread.

"Please, no," Ivette sobbed. "Not you. Please."

He swallowed the difficulty of witnessing Ivette in such a state. Tearful. Helpless. Frantic. And he highly suspected this was not the first time she'd gone through such a traumatic event.

They cleaned the cut, and Helen winced and muttered unintelligibly. Senna started stitching up the wound, and Ivette paced back and forth, back and forth across the small room.

Ben caught onto her hand and gave it a reassuring squeeze, offering what little comfort he could. Surprisingly, she latched on tight to his hand and gripped his arm with her other hand. It stopped her pacing, but her quivering didn't cease.

"It'll be alright," he murmured against her hair. "She'll be alright."

Helen blinked her eyes open the moment Senna cut the last thread. Ivette gasped and flew toward her little sister, holding her tight.

"They were trying to take the sheep," Helen croaked. "I tried to stop them."

Ivette smoothed the girl's hair down with her hand, and Ben took that moment to exit the room and storm outside into the chilly air of the oncoming storm.

He flexed his tight fingers as he searched the edge of the trees for any sign of the rustlers. He didn't know what he'd do if he found them, but he sure wanted to beat all three of them into a pulp. Helen could have died. Even sheep were dangerous if riled up enough.

He picked up a spade and tucked several rocks into his pocket beside the garden. Droplets of rain hit his face, but otherwise the storm was mild compared to what the dark clouds promised later in the evening.

The sheep bleated as he passed, some shivering from the fright and others shuffling their hooves with agitation. He gripped the wooden handle of the spade and ventured into the trees separating the fields from the unknown.

Going after the masked men was dangerous, especially considering he didn't know what weapons they might have on them, *and* they rode mounts.

He quickly learned he had exactly zero tracking skills, and he lost sight of the horses' hoofprints beneath the darkening skies. He returned to the fields before he managed to get himself lost, kicking a branch with the frustration that they'd gotten away. Sure, he'd injured a couple of the men. But it wasn't enough justice for stealing two sheep and almost killing a little girl.

Anger hardened on his face as he walked amongst the sheep with the spade tight in his hand, his gaze constantly scanning the area around them. The rustlers may have gotten two sheep, but he refused to allow them to steal another.

And to think he was about to leave these women by their lonesome and travel to Edilann. They lived on their own. Who was there to protect them from thieves and rustlers and bandits with ill intent?

He remained outside for hours until the skies darkened, and the moon rose. Sprinkles of rain chilled him to the bone, but still he stayed with the sheep. If those men were out there, there was no chance they'd take any other livestock tonight.

Lily called him inside for supper, but he waved her away and continued making his rounds in the fields.

Another hour passed, and he fought the weary exhaustion weighing on his shoulders. Clearly, he hadn't been one to stay on his feet all day in his past life, nor was he accustomed to life with a spade in his hand, as he was starting to feel blisters forming on his palm. He had fantastic aim with rocks and knives, he could ride a horse, and he could charm people into giving him what he wanted.

What kind of person possessed such skills? He seemed more at ease with solving problems and charming others than he was with manual tasks.

The sudden touch of a hand on his arm startled him, and he spun around, ready to face a potential threat. But his heart slowed when he found himself gazing back at Ivette, pleading in her expression.

"Come inside," she requested in a soft tone. "It's unlikely that they'll be back during the night if they haven't returned by now."

"They've already taken two sheep."

"I know." Her face crumpled, but she latched tighter onto his sleeve. "Come inside. The sheep are still frightened, and they will remain close for the night. They will let us know if the rustlers return."

He glanced toward the sheep, the cottage, and then at Ivette. The clouds released more of their pent-up rain, dripping onto the freckles across her nose and cheeks as she gazed back at him in the darkness. He recalled the way she'd picked up the shovel and charged after the rustlers, ready to fight off the threat with her own two hands. She was capable. Brave. And beautiful in every sense of the word.

But a vulnerability also lived within her eyes, as if her strength was fading, replaced by exhaustion and fear.

Finally, he nodded, and he followed her inside the cottage where a fire burned in the hearth to chase away the chill of the rainy night. All was still, as if everyone else had gone to bed, and she'd waited up for him.

She handed him a bowl of vegetable stew, and for a moment, her fingers lingered over his, as if she needed his strength when she was wilting before his eyes.

She dropped her hands, and it was all he could do to keep himself from snatching them back. Despite the hunger of a long night, he set the bowl on the kitchen table and led her toward the fire to warm herself. He sat in one of the chairs, but she remained standing, blinking rapidly while gazing into the flames.

The logs crackled and popped against the backdrop of rain pounding against the shingles of the roof.

"How is she?" he asked to break the silence in the room.

"She'll be fine. Just...quite the scare." More rapid blinking. "I don't know what would have happened if you hadn't been there."

He ducked his head to stare into his lap. "I wish I had acted faster."

"You saved her life." She paused and bit her lip. "I never got the chance to apologize for being short with you earlier." She moved closer to his chair and released a long breath. "My father left us in dire circumstances." Then she swiped her sleeve across her eyes. "My mother got trampled by horses years ago, and I cared for her until she eventually died. I thought Helen would suffer the same fate."

She wiped her eyes again.

Wordlessly, he took her hand and pulled her onto his lap. She gasped in surprise, at least until he pushed her face into his shoulder. She held still for several long moments before her shoulders began shaking, and she sobbed into his shirt.

He swallowed against the rising emotion stuck in his throat.

"I'm so tired," she wept. "These are my sisters, but I feel like I'm their mother. I do so much. I take on so much of the burdens they have no idea about! Financially, we are ruined. I don't know what to do, Ben. I just don't know what to do."

He stroked her long, soft hair, slightly damp from the rain, and frowned at her pain. "What about the money you get from the wool?"

She shook her head and sniffed. "My father took out a loan from a lender in my mother's name and ran away with the money and another woman." Another sniff. "I fled with my sisters to another kingdom to give us more time, but without money, I had to take out a loan from a different lender to pay for the house and sheep." She clutched onto his shirt and continued sobbing into his shoulder. "I can't do this, Ben. I can't shoulder this anymore. I can't keep my sisters housed and fed."

"It shouldn't have to be your responsibility," he murmured into her hair.

"But it is."

"What can I do? I have no name. No money. Well, not much, at least. And nothing but the clothes on my back. Yet, I will do anything to help shoulder your burdens." He tucked a strand of hair behind her ear as she lifted her face from his shoulder until they were only an arm's width apart. "What can I do for you?"

"Stay," she whispered. "The rustlers might return. Stay. To protect us and our livestock."

He blew out a long breath.

If he stayed, he might lose the chance to discover his identity. That, and he risked the girls' reputation being an unmarried man staying on a property filled with unmarried women. But he cared about this family. He cared about *her*. And he didn't care what anyone else might think of the situation.

"I will."

More tears fell from her eyes. Firelight flickered across her face, creating alluring shadows over her cheeks and mouth. His gaze dropped to her lips. He swallowed when an overwhelming desire for her burned in his chest. But he refused to take any liberties with her. Not when—

He grunted in surprise when she threaded her fingers through his hair and kissed him.

And like any foolish, besotted man, he couldn't resist her.

"Ivette," he whispered against her lips, drinking in the sweet taste of her mouth, her intoxicating scent, her warm fingers on his face, his neck, in his hair.

He tenderly cradled her face in his hands as he eagerly returned her kiss. Her skin was soft and smooth against his palms, and her hair was silky as he trailed the length of her tresses over her neck, shoulders, down her back to her waist.

An intoxicating, heady desire filled every breath with longing as he kissed her lips, her jaw, her neck. His hands traveled over her thighs, up her waist, and his finger traced the outline of the ties of her corset. He caught one of the loose strings between his fingers and pulled until the top loosened the slightest bit.

He sighed as his desire built up within him. His hands moved to her back. But the moment he touched the bare skin of one of her shoulders where the sleeve draped off one side, he froze when he realized what he was doing. What he knew with a sickening realization that he'd done many times in the past. But this time… He couldn't.

It took every ounce of what little self-control he possessed to release her one finger at a time, finding it extremely difficult to force his hand to drop from her shoulder and rest on the chair cushion to his side.

Not Ivette.

Not like this.

She certainly noticed his actions and seemed to mistake his intentions as she broke the kiss and pushed herself off his lap.

"I'm sorry!" she gasped. "I shouldn't have…I shouldn't have done that."

She hastily fixed her sleeve and quickened her pace down the hallway until her bedroom door closed with a click.

Ben rested his head on his hand as his gaze lingered on the darkened hallway long after she disappeared. Despite his earlier abominable realization, an unfamiliar warmth burned in his chest, one he knew without a doubt he had never felt before despite his loss of memory.

He was falling in love with Ivette Danvers.

Chapter Seven

"*G*ood morning, Grace!" Ben called to her sister where she sat reading by the fire as he entered the cottage the next morning, followed by a whistling tune before he set a pail of milk on the table.

Ivette's throat constricted, and her heart pounded at his sudden, unexpected appearance. She averted her gaze and stirred the fresh fruit in the pan faster in the process of making jam preserves.

She hadn't planned on kissing him last night. Truly. But he'd saved her sister, who was currently outside feeding the chickens after much insistence. The fire had created such a romantic atmosphere. And he'd smelled oh so good, like minty soap and something uniquely Ben...

The thought caused her face to burn, and she stirred even faster.

Ben continued to whistle, and she peeked over her shoulder to find him scooping the cream from the top of the milk like she'd taught him days ago.

His whistling transitioned into quiet singing, and she couldn't help but smile. He held the tune just fine, but his voice was average at best. Somehow, that relieved her, as his physique was too perfect for him to have a voice of gold to match. It made him more…human.

A contented sigh escaped her as she recalled the way he'd kissed her. With such skill and attentiveness. Soft and sweet with barely restrained passion.

Her entire body stiffened as his footsteps approached from behind, and his soft singing transitioned into an intimate chorus she almost felt was meant for her.

"And we sang, and we danced, and I kissed the prettiest girl in the village by the best happenstance."

Only then did she realize she'd stopped stirring enough for the mixture to bubble and spit. She continued her efforts, but she couldn't stop herself from turning her head to meet Ben's smiling gaze. He stopped singing long enough to kiss her cheek.

She inhaled a sharp breath of surprise, but before she could utter a word, he crossed the room and retrieved his black leather gloves from beside the door. The lingering grin on his face told of his intentions to continue as they were. To kiss. To court…

She wanted it more than anything.

And that's when she realized her heart was already gone. She'd wanted to spare herself from the pain of his inevitable departure. But for now, he'd promised to stay. And so, her heart could remain intact for a little while longer.

"What's next on the sheep agenda?" he asked, and she barely managed to restrain her own smile.

"They need to be herded to the upper pasture to graze. It's not easy," she warned.

"It can't be that hard." He laughed and shook his head. "They're just sheep."

Not even a half hour later, she and her sisters stood outside, watching as Ben rode the horse and swore up a storm when the sheep only moved aside, parting for the horse rather than getting herded as a whole. Just when he managed to urge half of the flock one way, the other half moved in the opposite direction.

"Should we help him?" Lily asked with a giggle just as Ben growled and swore again, clearly forgetting his current company.

Ivette shook her head, thinking of their father and his terrible relationship with their mother. "I want to see how he is when he's angry." Perhaps nothing would come of their budding relationship, but she wanted to be cautious before stepping into any sort of courtship.

"For the love!" Ben groaned, throwing his hands up in the air.

This time, Helen giggled, in much better spirits than the day before. Thankfully, the wound wasn't as bad as it had first appeared, unlike Ben's wound that had wiped his memories clean from his brain.

Senna elbowed her in the ribs. "I saw that kiss this morning."

She gasped and elbowed her sister right back. "You saw nothing. It didn't mean anything."

Lily rolled her eyes and sighed. "I wish he looked at me the way he looks at you. At this pace, I will become an old spinster living by myself in a cottage in the woods."

"You are nineteen years old," Senna pointed out before she frowned and tugged one of the ribbons out of Lily's hair. "That's mine."

"No, it's not." Lily snatched it back. "It was in my things."

"I bought it with my pin money. And this, too." Senna tugged a second ribbon from Lily's hair until the braid fell out and her hair tumbled around her shoulders.

Lily scowled. "Well, you are wearing my shawl." And then she grabbed the white knitted shawl and draped it around her own shoulders.

Senna glared moments before she flicked Lily's nose.

"Ow!" Lily cradled her nose and glared right back. She opened her mouth to likely spew out something else when Ivette stepped in.

"Today is supposed to be a somewhat peaceful and relaxing day." She gestured to the cloudless sky and the dry, green grass. "We'll have a picnic." And then her mouth twitched with humor as she glanced Ben's way, his frustration with his task showing clearly on his face. "And we'll enjoy the show."

"Are you sure we shouldn't help him?" Grace hugged her book close as she glanced toward him with a concerned pinch of her mouth.

"He'll manage." Though, she'd step in if he floundered too badly. A part of her hoped a bit of time on a horse might trigger his memories. Surely, there must be something that would help heal his mind from his traumatic fall.

They collected blankets, light refreshments, books, and hairbrushes and sat down beneath the shady trees creating a small clearing large enough for the five of them.

By the time Grace sat in front of her while she smoothed out her hair from its tie, Ben crossed the space from the barn to the clearing. To her surprise, the sheep now grazed at the upper pasture, and the horse likely resided in the barn.

Guilt lay on Ben's face as he approached, and then he grimaced as he glanced at each one of them. "I apologize for my language. I have learned I can sometimes frustrate easily. But from here on out, I will try to have more patience with difficult tasks."

Ivette's lips parted, and her hands stilled over Grace's dark tresses. Their mother had always said, *"Never trust a man who doesn't know how to apologize."*

Clearly, apologizing made him uncomfortable, but he'd done it. And all things considered, he hadn't gotten angry enough for concern. At least, he handled it fairly well. Aside from the cursing, of course.

She smiled and nodded her head to the empty space on the blanket beside Helen. "Come join our picnic."

"You can sit by me!" Helen cried, patting the space beside her. "Do you know how to braid hair? Can you braid mine?"

"Uhh…" He chuckled sheepishly and lowered himself onto the blanket. Ivette couldn't help but trail his movements. "I'm not entirely sure. But I can venture a confident guess that the answer would be no."

"It's not too hard," Lily said with a smile. "I'll show you."

As she did Grace's hair, Ivette couldn't help herself from stealing glances at the adorable way he puckered his mouth when he concentrated, the way he tipped his head as if the simple action could fix the mess he was making with Helen's hair.

He finished tying it off with a bow at the bottom of the braid and grimaced. The ensemble looked like a disaster with a tangle of knots and stray hairs sticking up in many places. "You just gotta… Put flowers in it." He plucked a few flowers from the base of the tree beside him and tucked them into Helen's hair. "See? It looks fine."

Ivette laughed, and he lifted his head to meet her eye, giving her a flirtatious grin that managed to tie her stomach in knots similar to Helen's messy hair.

"Look!" Helen exclaimed, breaking their attention apart as she picked up a white dandelion for herself and one for Ben. "It's a wish!"

Her little sister blew hers out quite messily, with a bit of spittle flying from her mouth. But then Ben blew on his. She watched as the small puffs of dandelion floated through the air, twirling with the faint breeze. Several of them landed directly on her lap. Her heart pounded as the two of them locked gazes once again, a special and meaningful understanding passing between them. They shared a connection. And she wanted to find out where that connection led.

He addressed all of them, but he only looked at her as he spoke. "During my exciting sheep-herding adventures, it got me thinking… All of you are good at making things pretty. I'm good at organizing things."

She lifted an eyebrow. "You're sure?"

"Allow me to rephrase that." He laughed and shook his head at her. "I *think* I'm good at organizing things. Let's have a ball. Here in the field. We'll invite the whole town with a small fee to get into the party. We'll have music and dancing and decorations—"

"And drinks!" Lily cried.

He swallowed, and his good humor instantly fell at the mention. Ivette watched as his mouth formed a tight smile. "And drinks. It will be a night to remember. We'll earn enough to make a hefty loan payment."

Her hand flew to her heart as she stared at him, trying to find out if this was only a game to him or if he truly meant it. But only earnestness lived in his eyes. He clearly wanted to help them, even though they weren't his responsibility.

"I thought we were almost paid off on the loan," Senna said, eyebrows furrowed.

"Loans," she corrected, staring shamefully into her lap. "The loaner stopped by last week. Says we have to make a half payment by the end of the month. Otherwise, he'll start seizing our property."

"Oh."

Everyone's mood deflated at the direness of their situation. Even though Ivette wanted to spare them, they needed to understand the full extent of their circumstances. "It's only a matter of time before the first loaner finds us as well. John Mavis lived in Edilann, and I heard he passed a year ago. It likely won't be long before the lord's heir finds us in his stead."

"Who is the heir?" Lily asked in a small voice.

Ivette shook her head. "I don't know his name."

Ben snapped his fingers, his gaze intense. "Mavis, Mavis, Mavis. I know that name."

"Vincent said you likely hailed from Edilann. Perhaps you know of them."

"So…" Senna crossed her arms. "We are utterly ruined."

"Unless we have nothing to give, we are not ruined. We have a week to come up with these funds to pay off half the loan. Ben has proposed a wonderful idea. I truly think this could work."

"But… Where will we get the things we need? Music? None of us play an instrument."

Standing up, Ben waved to all of them with a flourish of his hand. "Like I said, leave the organization to me. You ladies focus on refreshments and presentation. I will find musicians, get the word out in town, and find whatever else we need to make this a success."

Ivette gaped. "Who were you in your past life?"

He grabbed onto her hands and pulled her to her feet. She couldn't help but shriek with laughter when he spun her around and dipped her low enough for the ends of her hair to brush the ground.

"Perhaps a prince." He waggled his eyebrows.

"You would have been found by now." She laughed and playfully swatted his shoulder when he placed her upright.

"A cobbler," he guessed again. "I have nice shoes." But then he grimaced as everyone's attention pulled to the dirt and grass-stained boots threatening to fall apart more each day. "I *had* nice shoes."

"Oh! Oh!" Helen's hand waved wildly through the air. "A scribe! Your handwriting is lovely."

Ben snapped his fingers and pointed to her. "Now we're on the right track. I was a live-in scribe at a wealthy house, and when they were about to place my head beneath the chopper, I stole their clothes and horse and ended up in Avorstead."

Ivette's face blanched but Helen giggled and continued the pretend story enthusiastically. "You forgot the part where you rescued the fair maiden from the chopper as well, and the two of you ran away and lived happily ever after."

He laughed and pulled the small girl into a side embrace. "If the story ends happily, I'm content enough."

Surreptitiously, he turned his head and winked at Ivette, and in response, her face heated as it always did when he gave her special attention. She could easily imagine him already having broken dozens upon dozens of hearts. But she was glad hers wouldn't become one of them. Because she was sure he returned her feelings.

The faintest smile turned her lips upward, and she shifted her body to hide it. She was looking forward to the upcoming "ball" more than he could possibly know.

Chapter Eight

Between daily chores and planning for the upcoming ball in the fields in only five days, Ben had never been so busy since he woke from hitting his head. He tried his best to help with the heavy lifting around the farm, and he also spent a lot of time in town with small errands while simultaneously getting other townsfolk excited about the ball.

So far, they'd received nothing but enthusiasm over the event, even when it required a fee to get in. But others were hesitant, and those were the ones he focused on helping out in town to try to gain more interest. The girls could use every bit of money they could get.

And besides, this was supposed to be fun for everyone.

He stood in the barn, saddling Brith as if he'd done the task thousands of times in his past life. Blanket. Saddle. Straps. Bridle. The familiar task was a balm to his soul, making a foreign world not quite so foreign and terrifying.

What if I never remember?

The voice inside his head caused him to frown as he finished strapping the bridle around Brith's ears. It was very possible he would never recover his memories. In such an instance, he would need to find work, a place to stay other than sleeping in the barn, and he'd need the means of supporting himself when he possessed nothing but a pocket watch, a small knife, and the clothing on his back.

Starting at the bottom sounded like a daunting task. But at this point, it might be necessary.

In his distraction, he startled at the brush of something against his hand. Ivette placed a folded letter inside his palm, gave him a coy, heart-stopping smile, and disappeared just as quickly.

And like any besotted man, he hurried to unfold the paper. A silly smile took over his entire face as he read the letter.

Dear Ben (?),

I've not had the chance to speak with you in far too long. And yes, a couple days is far too long. In a house full of sisters, there is no such thing as privacy.

I wanted to express my appreciation for what you have been doing for our family. It might not be much to you, but it's everything to us. You have given us hope, but especially me, for a brighter future unladen with so much burden. If only you had conked your head on our property years ago. I would not have minded so much to have had you around sooner.

Here's to the hope that we might see one another somewhere other than the dining table.
Always,
Ivette

He strode to the barn entrance in search of her, but to his dismay, he spotted her with Grace, the two of them pulling up vegetables from the garden. If it was a moment alone she wanted, then he'd happily force open a bit of room in their busy schedules. Pry it open if he had to.

His grin lingered as he stuffed the letter into his pocket. Of all the cliffs to fall off of, he was glad he'd fallen off hers.

Mounting the horse with a single swoop of his leg, he reined her out of the barn and onto the road leading to town. Dust kicked up on the road and tickled his nose. The sunshine blazed down on him, warming his back as he traveled. People on the road waved and greeted him by name, and he did his best to recall their names as well.

Warmth buried itself in his heart. The seed of happiness blossomed within him. Even if he never recovered his memories, he couldn't think of a place he wanted to be that might make him happier than he was now.

When he reached town, he traded and bartered and spent a lot of time getting to know the townsfolk, even helping them with odd jobs here and there to get them to like him more, and in turn, get them interested in the event in five days.

Several musicians volunteered their talents to the cause in exchange for a free admission. Others volunteered to bring food and decorations. The ball was going to have a large turnout, and he admitted he was looking forward to the look on Ivette's face when guests arrived by the bucketful with payment in hand.

Ben finished loading a crate into the back of the mercantile owner's wagon when the man, Blain, rounded the side, his face red with exertion.

"I'm still not sure…" the man said with hesitance in his tone. "The cost is small, but for a party in this economy?"

Ben stepped closer and lowered his voice. "Truth be told, the girls will be turned out of their home if they can't raise enough money in the next week. They've been on their own for so long…" He hefted a long sigh and shook his head.

Lowering his voice as well, Blain replied, "I didn't know their circumstances were so dire. Of course, none of the girls have succeeded in finding a husband without a dowry. Otherwise, I'm sure their fortunes would look up."

"No one in town is interested?" He picked at his already clean nails, trying to sound nonchalant when in reality, his heart pounded as he waited to find out if he had any competition for Ivette's affection.

Blain laughed. "What unattached young man *isn't* interested in courting the dames? But times are tough, and those who have dowries are chosen for wives over those who don't."

He huffed at the ludicrous idea. The girls were plenty beautiful and talented, even without such dowries to aid them in securing a good match.

His head ached so suddenly as to jar him into taking a stumbling step backward. His head spun. His ears rang. Something flitted on the edge of his memory. Darkness. Confusion. Frustration.

"Ben?" The voice echoed somewhere far away. "Ben?"

The darkness slowly dissipated until he found himself sitting on the ground, his back resting against the large wheel of a wagon. Blain crouched before him, fanning his face with a dirtied white cloth.

"You just about passed out there. You gonna be alright?"

A lingering ache pounded in his temple, and he blinked several times to chase it away. Heat climbed his neck when he realized an audience had witnessed his lapse of bodily control. Several people stood across the road with concerned expressions, whispering to one another.

Don't show weakness, his mind whispered to him. *You will be mocked and ridiculed.*

He grasped Blain's outstretched hand and forced himself to remain steady on his feet rather than topple over. His stomach heaved at the sudden motion. But he smiled tightly through the nausea.

"A long day on my feet is all," he lied. He clapped the man on the back. "See you at the party?"

Blain heaved a sigh, his gaze finding his two daughters and two sons in front of the mercantile chattering excitedly about the ball. "Count on the five of us." Another sigh as he placed his hands on his hips. "I can't sell the stock we recently received, as they're considered damaged goods. But they're good enough to drink. We'll bring a few casks of ale."

Ben's throat tightened. His teeth clenched. His nostrils flared as a dreadful desire squeezed him until he barely managed to draw air into his lungs. Shame pricked at him like a hot needle. Self-hatred quickly followed.

Whatever he'd done in his past, it must not be good when his subconscious was wary of the drink. He'd avoid it at all costs.

He nodded, teeth still clenched. "The Danvers sisters will appreciate your contribution."

To shake the feeling of addicting desire, he located his mount secured to the hitching post and swung himself into the saddle. The horse snorted, ears flicking back as if she sensed the tension in his body.

Whatever this was, he'd get through it. Because surely it would get easier to handle with each passing day. Surely.

After another two days passed of no privacy, no time alone, and very little free time, Ivette was strung tight after all the longing glances between herself and Ben, the lingering stares, the subtle winks, the letters passed back and forth. Some silly. Others flirty and romantic. She'd catch him watching her when she tended to the sheep, and he'd catch her watching as he hefted hay and crates of apples.

It was a shame he slept in the barn rather than the front room of the cottage now. But it was also for the best for the sake of all their reputations.

When Ben didn't show up to supper, disappointment turned her blood cold. A pit of uncertainty dropped to her stomach. Her heart beat a sad rhythm within her chest. She couldn't help but question…was it all in her head? Yes, Ben flirted with anything wearing a skirt, but she suspected it was just his personality rather than a conscious effort on his end. Especially because he also flirted with the matrons of the town. They loved it. They loved him. Everyone loved him.

And she was not immune herself.

As she washed the dishes from supper in the frigid water in the sink, she rubbed a damp hand over her aching heart. It did not bode well for her to dwell on frilly things like ribbons and dresses and romance. It was unlike her to allow a handsome face to distract her from her work, but her heart had other ideas.

A knock sounded on the door, startling her into splashing water across her dress. She quickly dried her hands and crossed the kitchen to the door. But as the hinges creaked when she opened it, she frowned when no one stood on the opposite side.

She glanced back and forth across the darkening fields, trying to convince herself the knock hadn't been only in her head.

She started to close the door when she spotted a folded piece of parchment lying on the doormat. Curiosity piqued, she stooped to pick it up, only for her heart to hammer against her ribs when she recognized the elegant scrawl across the page as she unfolded it.

Ivette,

The moon is white. The fields are green. Meet me in the place where the branches lean.
B

Her pulse raced as she threw her apron onto the back of a kitchen chair and smoothed down the flyaways of her hair. She stopped for a moment to listen as her sisters laughed and screeched and argued, their voices muffled by the doors down the hallway.

No one would notice if she slipped away for a bit...would they?

Oh, who was she kidding? They would notice. And they'd know exactly where she'd gone. But she couldn't bring herself to care. Because for years, she had looked after their happiness and their well-being. Perhaps it was now time to look after her own.

Smoothing down her clothing one last time, she stepped outside into the darkness and closed the door quietly behind her. She glanced around, noting the dark silhouette of the trees, the fade of blue in the sky where the sun disappeared behind the horizon, the specks of white dotting the lower field where the sheep grazed.

Where do the branches lean? she asked herself while surveying the landscape. In the orchard, the apple tree branches leaned a bit too close together, as she hadn't found the time to prune them this year.

Chunks of wood rested under a large cloth in the shed.

The tree on the hill—

A nervous excitement alighted in her chest when she recalled the large branches they'd collected from the upper field after a storm had ripped them from the trees. They'd leaned the branches against one of the larger trees near the cliffside to take care of them later.

She forced herself into a steady gait as she climbed the hill toward the tree in question. Her heart squeezed anxiously when she spotted Ben leaning casually against the trunk, his arms crossed in an easygoing manner. He wore his white shirt tucked into his dark, fitted trousers, the sleeves rolled up to the elbows and the first two buttons unfastened to reveal the dip of his chest.

I can't do this, she told herself as panic spurred her heart faster.

She didn't know what *this* was, but it terrified her. It made her want to simultaneously crumple into a heated puddle and flee back down the hill.

But then he set her at ease with a soft smile and friendly eyes. Her heart calmed. Her body relaxed. And the previous excitement returned when she realized it was just Ben. The same Ben she had dragged unconscious behind a horse. The same Ben who helped them with daily chores and their financial burdens. The same Ben who protected them and spent time with them and laughed with them around the dining table.

Her Ben.

"You liked my poem?" His teeth gleamed white in the darkness as he grinned. "I was thinking about it all day. I thought myself clever."

"Oh, I've read cleverer poems," she replied coyly when her desire to flee turned in the opposite direction entirely. But then she gasped as he grabbed onto her waist and pulled her closer until only a small gap rested between them.

"I have another one for you." The silkiness of his voice caressed her cheek and sent a pleasant shiver down her spine. "Her hair is like the sunset gold. Eyes like the springtime thaw. Ivette is incredible, and I'm in complete awe."

She swallowed before releasing a raspy breath. "You say that to all the girls."

He chuckled lightly and released her for only a moment to gesture around them. "What girls? I have an enormous pit in my memories. If there were other girls, I certainly don't remember them."

"And were you thinking of that one all day, too?"

"Nah. I made it up on the spot. Not bad, right?"

Her mouth twitched as she fought a smile but ended up losing when he held her with tender hands and smiled at her with the sweetest gaze. "You are a complete mystery, Ben."

"I absolutely agree with your comment. I'm learning plenty of new things about myself every day."

Her breath hitched as he trailed his fingers through her hair and then picked up a strand, bringing it to his lips for a lingering kiss. He picked up her hand next, and she was grateful to the darkness for hiding her furious blush when he kissed her knuckles next, and then flipped her hand over to press an intimate kiss to her wrist.

He didn't kiss her again like she hoped he might, but rather wrapped his arms around her shoulders and pulled her into an embrace. He released a long sigh and held her tighter.

"Is something the matter?" she asked, steeling herself for an answer she might not like.

However, he shook his head. "Being near you like this… It feels like coming home."

Emotion pricked at Ivette's eyes, and she finally gained the courage to lift her arms and return his embrace around the waist. Holding him was terrifying. Because she feared she might lose him if she let go. And she didn't want to lose him.

She loved him.

Admitting the words in her mind caused her pulse to thrum in her veins, faster and faster with each moment she held him. During the past few weeks, he'd easily captured her heart and held it with tender hands. She should have known her heart was well on its way to falling the moment she spotted him on that cliff. He'd left a permanent imprint on her heart that even the strongest of soaps couldn't scrub away.

Releasing a contented sigh, she rested her head against his sturdy chest and reveled in the strength of his arms around her. She couldn't imagine a life without him in it.

He was…

…family.

She smiled into his shirt and held on tighter.

"I asked you up here to stargaze," he murmured against her hair. "But this is nice, too."

She turned her head slightly and spotted the blanket spread across the grass, giving them a great view of the sky overhead. But she knew an even better view.

Laughing, she grabbed his hand and pulled him toward the trunk of the tree, releasing him only to latch onto one of the lower branches and pull herself up. Her experienced feet easily climbed branch after branch, her expert hands guiding her upward.

"What are you doing?" Ben called up from below.

"You'll have to follow me to find out!" she shouted back.

He grunted as he climbed the first branch, and he barely caught himself as his foot slipped. For a moment, her heart dropped as she recalled with perfect clarity when he'd fallen from the cliff that fateful night only to lay on the ground unmoving.

Ben chuckled wryly as he struggled up to the next branch, awkwardly folding himself over the tree limb. "I'm embarrassed to admit that I don't think I'm much of a climber."

"Really?" she asked sarcastically, arching her eyebrow.

"I know, I know. I'm better at falling than climbing. But it's the effort that counts, no?" Still, he gave a valiant effort to follow her until they stood on the same branch sturdy enough to support both their weight, him a head taller than her.

The small space forced them close together until his heat seeped into her, and she didn't think she could place distance between them even if she tried. She wanted him near enough to touch, to view the softness of his smile, the caring in his eyes.

"If you wanted to get real snug, we could have done so on the ground," he teased.

She lightly smacked his arm, afraid anything more might cause him to lose his balance and topple the distance to the earth. "Turn around."

A question lingered in his eyes as he did as she asked, and she smiled when he inhaled sharply.

From their vantage point, they had a view of the entire valley. The stars twinkling above. The silhouette of the mountains against the dark blue backdrop of the sky. The endless stretch of trees and fields and rivers.

The view stole her breath away. The peacefulness of the atmosphere settled all the doubts and fears in her heart.

But after Ben continued to stare silently at the horizon, she glanced at his face to find a somber sadness in his expression.

"Ben?" she murmured, placing her hand on his arm. Only then did he tear his gaze away and settle his attention on her. The turmoil in his eyes tied her stomach into an uneasy knot.

"I can't chase away the fear that… What if I'm a bad person?" His throat bobbed with a swallow. "I catch…glimpses of myself, of who I might have been. And…"
A pause. "And I'm terrified of what I might find on the other end."

She took a hold of his hand and squeezed, trying to convey her sincerity with her eyes. "You lost all your memories of your past. Strip all of that away, and you are a good man. *This*," she placed her hand over his heart and felt its steady rhythm against her palm, "is who you are. Whatever your history looks like, it's not your true self. What you decide to do in the present matters more than the demons of the past."

He placed a hand over hers, and they remained in that position for several long beats of silence, until a flicker of a grin returned to his mouth. "So, you're saying if I made my living as a rustler stealing sheep from beautiful women, perhaps you might still like me?"

"Oddly specific." She laughed and rolled her eyes. "If you continued to do such a thing, I would be very displeased with you. But the past is in the past." And then she nudged him with her elbow. "I think I'd even like you if you couldn't climb trees."

The cross look he gave her almost encouraged her mouth to split into a grin, but she was determined to hold her ground this time and challenged him with a stare.

"Alright, so I'm not great at tree climbing." His gaze dropped to her lips. "But there is something else I'm quite good at."

The new issued challenge took her off guard, and her heart responded with a flurry of racing activity. "I wish I could deny it just to wipe the smug grin from your face."

He shrugged, and his wicked smirk grew wider. "There are other ways to wipe the smug grin from my face."

She didn't realize she'd clutched onto the front of his shirt until her fingers tightened their grip. She couldn't resist this man, and she didn't want to try. "I have no idea what you're talking about."

"Then I must remedy that." He shifted his body closer, his head dipping until their lips rested only a breath apart. But rather than closing the distance between them, he teased her by keeping himself just out of reach. She hadn't the breath to ask him to stop.

Her scalp received a gentle tug as he wrapped her long hair several times around his hand and pulled her head back to reveal the length of her throat. He kissed the spot between her shoulder and neck. She released a trembling breath.

"I could worship every single one of your freckles," he murmured against her skin, now trailing light kisses from her neck to her jaw.

"No one else has liked them," she managed in a raspy tone.

"No, no, no. I think you are mistaken." He kissed her beneath the ear. "I know this without a doubt despite the darkness of my past... We are not *supposed* to like them. Society tells us we want women with fine, unblemished skin. But..." He growled playfully and pulled her closer by the waist until their bodies were flush against one another. "I love them."

Love...

He didn't say he loved *her*, but she hoped with all her heart that he returned her feelings.

His tongue lightly traced the shell of her ear, and she couldn't help but gasp and cling tighter as he made her heady with longing.

"You were right," she breathed.

"About what?" Next, he nibbled on her earlobe, and her lightheadedness affected her balance. "I'm right about a lot of things."

Her laughter turned into another heavy breath as he tugged on her hair and kissed her jaw. "We should have *stargazed* on the ground."

"You are jesting if you think I can get myself back down."

She laughed again, her heart warming with his humor. The best thing to have ever happened to her was this man coming into her life, and she wanted to keep him. Forever. "I love you, Ben."

She inhaled sharply when the words escaped past her wall of fortitude. They both stared back at each other, wide-eyed, no words. Now, if *that* wasn't a glass of cold water dumping over her head after the heat of his fiery kiss, she didn't know what was.

"A-a-ahh… I m-m-mean…"

But he stopped her stammering with a sweet, gentle kiss against her lips, and her heart smoothed its frantic beat with calm relief. He pulled her closer, his hands roaming over her hair, her back, her waist. She smoothed her hands over his chest, daring to touch him as if he were a precious statue she didn't want to break.

Her confidence grew bolder as she trailed her hands up his chest, over his shoulders, and dug her fingers through his soft, silky hair. The way he kissed her with a gentle passion melted her heart into a puddle. Every touch. Every caress. Every kiss. They lit her blood on fire and then some. Yes, he certainly was quite good at this. Better than good, as he certainly had downplayed his talent despite his boasting.

He gave her one last lingering kiss, and when their lips parted, her eyes remained closed with complete rapture, with a mouth satiated and well-explored.

Yet, she wanted more. She wanted to kiss him until dawn made its appearance in the sky. To hold him until the nighttime chill set into her bones. To talk for hours about everything and nothing at the same time.

"I think I know my limits here," he said quietly as he brushed a whisper across her cheek with his lips. "I want more than anything to respect you."

A part of her told her it didn't matter because she loved him. Another part warned against giving him anything unless a further commitment was made. It was simply difficult when he kissed like *that*.

Her eyelids fluttered open as she sighed playfully. "Then I suppose I will be content enough with you worshiping every one of my freckles."

"Careful," he growled, pulling her closer until the minty scent of him filled every one of her senses. "Such worshiping will most definitely push me over my limits."

She laughed, her smile lingering as she picked up his hand and kissed his palm. "Then you will have to lay on one side of the blanket, and me on the other."

"Not a chance."

He tried to pull her into another kiss, but she ducked beneath his attempt and laughed as she climbed back down the tree, branch after branch, limb after limb. She reached the ground before him, of course, but surprisingly, his feet awkwardly hit the earth not long after.

True to his word, he gathered her into his arms as they lay on the blanket in the darkness beneath the shimmering stars.

He didn't kiss her again, and she didn't press him for more. She, too, wanted to respect him and his boundaries and prevent herself from tempting him further than he was able to manage.

With her head resting against his shoulder, she gazed at the sky above. A falling star shot across the inky canvas and disappeared in a brief flash of light.

"A falling star for good luck," she murmured, holding him even closer and nuzzling into his shoulder.

He kissed her temple. "I don't need luck when I have everything I want lying in my arms."

In a husky whisper, she repeated, "You say that to all the girls."

"There are no other girls. Only you."

Her heart warmed at the declaration, and she knew it to be true. He was a good, honest man, and she was lucky to have him. "Save me a dance at the ball?"

He pulled her closer. "I would selfishly take all your dances. But ballroom etiquette dictates I can have two but no more."

She leaned up on her elbow. "Ballroom etiquette? Where did you learn about that?"

He frowned, eyebrows drawn together. "I'm not sure."

"Do you think your memories are returning?"

"I don't think so." But then the worry creases in his forehead smoothed out as he smiled and brushed his thumb along her jaw. "Two dances. No more. No less."

Placing a gentle kiss on the corner of his mouth, her heart warmed at the way his lips responded with a smile. "I look forward to it."

Chapter Nine

The day finally arrived, and thus far, there was a bigger turnout at the dance than Ben had previously expected. Lively music lifted into the air. Laughter rang out on all sides of him. The sweet scent of cider and ale lingered closer to the table of refreshments. Colorful garlands of flowers stretched overhead next to an abundance of lanterns lighting up the space.

Skirts twirls. Smiles lit up each face. And for the life of him, Ben could hardly follow the movement as the townsfolk danced a series of line dances completely unfamiliar to him.

He wanted to join and perhaps even make a fool of himself as he tried to follow the quick steps, but…

A pounding ache formed in his temple. An incessant ringing attacked mercilessly in his ears. He barely managed to stay on his own two feet, and he might have toppled over long ago if it hadn't been for a fence keeping him upright.

Many people approached to talk to him, and he gave them an easy smile and lively conversation, remembering each by name or occupation.

But in reality, he wanted to lie down until the ringing dissipated and the headache ebbed. Clouded confusion erupted in his head. Flashes of anger, betrayal, and hopelessness echoed through the dark chambers of his mind. The silhouette of a sick man lying in bed. The quiet fear of a woman.

And then…

The tip of his finger brushed against his bare ring finger. He wasn't married in his past life. He knew it for certain. But there had been a woman.

She was a silhouette. No more. And layers upon layers of shame and self-hatred buried him with the faintest recollection of her memory.

What had he done to her for such strong feelings of shame to surface in his mind? Was he truly a livestock rustler like he feared, and he'd hurt her in some way?

He hung his head, his stare burning into the grass at his feet. He truly wanted to be a good man. But what if he wasn't? Ivette deserved nothing less.

At the thought of her, he lifted his head and his gaze roamed over the party guests until it landed on her. A slow smile lifted on his lips at her laughter as her partner swung her in quick circles on the dance floor before handing her off to another partner.

He watched, transfixed, as her copper hair flew behind her in a mesmerizing sheen. As her skirts twirled around her legs. As her pink lips smiled with complete joy. She was beautiful in every sense of the word.

I love you, too, he said in his mind as he watched her dance. *But I can't say it, and I don't know why.*

He heavily suspected he'd never said the words to a woman before. Not because he'd never had a chance. But because they were a serious declaration. A commitment. A way to allow himself to get hurt. He didn't like not being in control, and giving his heart to another person relinquished his control entirely.

Being near Ivette… He felt like he had very little control at all. And it frightened him.

A small, self-protecting part of him warned him to flee. Before their relationship became too serious. Before he had everything to lose.

Another part of him urged him to take action. Although his memories continued to flit out of reach, he still had *her*. They could get m…m…mmm…

He took a deep breath and forced himself to think the word. *Married.*

In Edilann, they had strict marriage laws, especially for the nobility. The king himself had to be married to remain on the throne. And it was frowned on in society should a member of nobility not be married past his twenty-fourth birthday.

The ringing in his ears grew louder as he realized that bit of information was new, something pulled from the pit of his memories.

But before he had a chance to dwell more on it, a familiar voice boomed across the yard, and the mercantile owner approached with a hearty wave.

"Ah, Ben!" Blain slapped him on the back in greeting. "Woulda told you sooner, but I didn't see you till now." His voice slurred, betraying what lay inside the tankard he held and how much he'd already consumed. "Three fellas came by lookin' for you."

Ben furrowed his brows. "For me? Someone in town?"

The man shook his head. "Three chaps from Edilann, I reckon. Their accent was similar to yours." He hiccupped, all while Ben's heart beat faster and faster with disbelief. "Well, they didn't ask for *you* per say. They were lookin' for a man named…" He frowned and scratched his chin. "I don't remember the name they said. But it started with a B."

"How do you know they were looking for me then?"

"One said he saw you in the sheep fields and was askin' round town where to find you."

A frozen cold dread burned in his belly as he recalled the rustlers and the man with the familiar face. How did the man know him?

"A-a-and…" Ben blew out a long breath. "And what did you tell them?"

"They looked like the no-gooder sort." Hiccup. "I told 'em don't know anybody by that name." Hiccup. Sway. "To try the next town over."

Ben ran his fingers through his hair, staring at the long, dark road leading toward the town as he struggled to comprehend what this meant. People were looking for him. But who were they? And how was he associated with the thieves?

One thing he knew for sure… He needed to find them before they came back to the fields and terrorized the Danvers girls again.

Clapping the other man on the shoulder, Ben said, "If they come around again, make sure to let me know." *Hopefully a bit quicker next time.*

"Mmhmm." Hiccup. "You look parched. Have a drink!" Blain shoved a tankard of ale into his chest, the liquid slopping over his shirt.

It took every bit of his self-control to keep his hands by his sides, especially as the aroma fused into his clothing and threatened to seize his wits. He breathed in deeply and released the breath, but the smell clung to his nose, making it impossible to ignore the call of the drink.

At the moment, he wanted it more than anything. To take the edge off his escalating fear. To bury him in unwavering elation until every worry dissipated beneath the heady atmosphere of music, laughter, and excitement.

But the thought of Ivette kept his wits grounded enough to push the tankard away. "I don't drink."

Yet, his throat burned with need. His mouth salivated with want. His mind begged for a sip—just a taste. Surely, a small sip wouldn't hurt.

No!

A warning bell blared inside his head. Although he didn't remember what might happen if he gave into the temptation, he knew he didn't want to find out.

Again, he shook his head and stepped back.

Blain shrugged with indifference and chugged the rest of the tankard, releasing a loud belch before swaying on his feet. "Can't believe I couldn't sell this batch," he slurred again. "It's the best," hiccup, "I've ever tasted."

The man disappeared into the crowd, and Ben longingly glanced toward the casks of ale he'd purposely been avoiding all night.

To take his attention away from his temptation, he approached the musicians after the song ended and requested one of his own. A slower tune lifted into the night, giving many dancers a much-needed rest.

He strode toward Ivette where she laughed and spoke animatedly to a friend from town. When their eyes locked, the world around him disappeared, and he lost himself in a sea of beautiful hazel. Torchlight flickered off her face, squeezing every bit of air from his lungs until he struggled to breathe.

His mind refused to behave tonight, and along with the flashes from his past, he saw *her*. The determination in her eyes when she'd fought to keep him alive. The fear when he'd struggled to pull through his injuries. The relief when he'd woken.

He knew without a doubt he'd never met anyone like her in his life. And he decided then that he'd do whatever it took to keep her.

As he stopped in front of her, he held out a hand, palm up. "Would you honor me with a dance, Miss Danvers?"

She giggled at his formality and slipped her fingers into his. "I'd love to, Sir Ben."

The moment he grasped her hand, he twirled her onto the dance floor, overly aware of dozens of eyes on them, watching their every move.

The steps came easily as he led her in a dance in sync with the beat of the music. He moved forward, she moved back. He moved back, she moved forward. All the while, he held her gaze, hoping to convey the workings of his heart not with words but with all the heartfelt emotion in his eyes.

He twirled her again, her skirts fanning out around her before she spun back to his side and her hand found his again.

Although she clearly didn't know the steps to the dance, his heart warmed as she placed her trust in him to guide her through the steps with fluidity and grace.

They ended with a twirl before he bowed over her hand and kissed her fingers.

"Now, that's some fancy folk dancing!" Vincent laughed, followed by loud clapping. Others whistled and clapped around them. Ivette's face lit up with a bright blush while he took the unexpected attention in stride, bowing several times at the waist. No one else had joined them on the dance floor, giving them far too much attention than he'd wanted.

A pulsing ache throbbed once more at his temple, and he tried to hide it with a smile as he led Ivette off the dance floor.

"What is your secret?" she asked breathlessly.

"To what?" He squinted when the lights became too bright, and the music was too loud, and he didn't have enough room to breathe.

"To appear so…perfect."

His eyebrows shot up, and he mentally counted every one of his faults and struggles since they'd met all those weeks ago. Perfection lay far out of reach, but rather than mocking himself for his shortcomings, he grinned playfully. "One of the tricks to appear extraordinary is to play on your strengths and your assets, rather than emphasize what you lack."

"Like climbing trees," she jested.

He pinched her side, causing her to laugh out loud. "You won't see me attempting such a feat in front of an audience."

"But you tried with me."

His gaze softened as he turned her to face him and ran a strand of her hair between her fingers. "Because I trust you. I feel…safe with you."

"Ben…" She tipped her head until it rested against his hand.

The vulnerability he displayed created a discomforting pit in his stomach, followed by an excruciating pain now in the back of his head. He released her and placed his hand against his head instead.

"I don't feel well. I think I need to…sit down." Or rather lay down and sleep it off. But the girls had worked so hard to bring this party to fruition. He couldn't abandon them now.

"You pushed yourself too hard." She took his arm with gentle hands and led him toward an empty chair facing away from the lights.

"What about your second dance?" Bright lights continued to sear his eyes, and he dug his palms into his eye sockets to ward off the ache. The tempo of the music picked up once more, followed by laughter and dancing. It was too much. Too much light. Too much sound. Too many people.

Ivette placed her hand over his forehead as if in search of any signs of a fever. He didn't feel hot. But his head hurt more than it should. "You'll owe me one dance for later. I'll hold you to it."

The pain squeezing his head became too much to form a reply. He was vaguely aware of her disappearing from his side for a few minutes before returning with a glass of water and a tankard of cider.

He accepted the glass from her and downed the water in several long gulps. When the pain persisted, he reached for the tankard next. But as he lifted it to his lips, the smell of ale stung his nostrils, and he froze before the liquid touched his mouth.

"This isn't cider," he rasped.

She shook her head. "I've heard ale can help with headaches." She laughed and shook her head. "Maybe today but probably not tomorrow. Perhaps it might help take the edge off the pain."

I shouldn't...

But he wanted to.

How much could it truly hurt? Likely not any worse than the pounding in his skull. Besides, Ivette had his best interests at heart. She wouldn't do anything to hurt him.

And so, he gave in and took a sip.

One sip turned into two, which turned into three, then five. And soon enough, Ben lost himself in drink after drink, losing count after the fourth tankard of ale. His thoughts became jumbled, his speech slurred. He laughed more freely. Teased the young men. Flirted with the matrons. And with each passing moment of disorientation, he longed for Ivette, wanting her more than he wanted anything in the entire kingdom.

The night flashed in a blur as the liquor took control of him. One moment, he was dancing with Vincent's wife, and when he blinked, he found his mouth against the lip of a tankard. He blinked again and found himself stumbling toward the barn, following after a pretty head of copper hair.

A warning flashed in his mind, telling him to fight the effects of the ale. But he'd consumed so much that he could hardly control his sluggish limbs as he followed the flicker of light from the lantern she held in her hands.

"Where are we going?" he slurred, stumbling after her.

She jumped and spun around, a hand held to her heart. "Oh! Ben. You frightened me." But she didn't lift her pretty little lips into a smile. Rather, something akin to worry stared back at him.

"Grace has been in the barn for hours. I thought I should check on her. She doesn't like crowds."

He blinked again, and Ivette was pressed against him where he pinned her against the side of the barn, one arm above her head in the shadowy darkness.

Don't do this! his mind screamed at him. *You'll lose her. You'll lose her!*

He fought against the pull of the liquor running rampant through his body, through his mind. It blurred his thoughts. It poorly affected his rationale and intellect.

Losing control of his limbs, he gripped Ivette's wrist too hard, and she hissed. Her green eyes widened, and she pushed against his chest. "Ben, you've had too much to drink. You need to go lie down."

He shook his head to try to clear the fog from his thoughts. He blinked again, and his hand was cupped beneath her knee, her leg pressed against his.

"Stop." She pushed against his chest again.

The fog in his mind cleared enough for him to drop her leg and step backward. He never pursued a woman without her consent. But when his thoughts lay jumbled in his mind and his surroundings spun, it remained difficult to keep his hands to himself.

"Ivette," he slurred, taking a step toward her. But he misjudged the distance between them and accidentally kicked over the lantern at their feet.

Glass shattered. Dry grass caught fire. And within moments, the flames climbed the parched wood of the barn, fast and without mercy.

He stared dumbstruck at the growing flames, his mind too slow as he tried to figure out what to do. But beside him, Ivette reacted faster.

"Grace!" she gasped before rounding the barn and bursting through the doors.

Ben stumbled after her but tripped over his own foot and landed hard on the ground. Smoke burned his nostrils. Screams and shouts permeated the air. His mind buzzed and spun and ached, but Grace's scream from within the barn was like cold ice water dumping over his head, sobering him enough to climb to his feet and rush toward the sound.

Ivette supported a soot-covered Grace on one arm as she emerged from the barn, but distress lived in her eyes when she glanced backward. Only then did he realize someone else was in there.

Another scream.

Helen!

The heat of the flames seared his skin as he moved closer with the intent to enter the barn, but Vincent and another man rushed past him, far quicker on their feet, and entered the burning barn while others stood in a line, passing water-filled buckets between each other from the well to the building.

Not knowing what else to do, Ben joined the line closest to the fire and threw buckets of water on the flames, all while glancing toward the entrance. Vincent and Helen still hadn't emerged.

Please, he begged. *Please, please, please.*

The fire sizzled against the splash of water, but it still wasn't enough. But no one stopped their efforts, and he refused to either.

At last, Vincent burst out of the barn carrying Helen over his shoulder, while the other man held the reins of the horse and cow. The horse nickered nervously, but Ben watched Helen with horror in his eyes.

Soot covered the girl's skin, and a patch of her dress looked to have been burned and the flames quickly stamped out.

The moment they exited the barn, Helen slid from Vincent's arms and to the ground. She rushed into Ivette's embrace, and her sister proceeded to plant kisses over her face.

Relief filled him that not only was she alive, but she was well, too.

When the flames proved too much to combat, they dampened the grass around the barn before they all stood back and watched in silence as it burned. Wood splintered and crashed, sending up a plume of sparks and embers. Slowly, the fire ate away at the wood, turning the barn to ash, until nothing remained but a pile of charred lumber.

Ben's gaze turned to Ivette to find Vincent's wife, Elinor, comforting her with an arm around her shoulders.

"It's alright," Ivette said loudly for everyone to hear. "We can build a new barn. I'm only glad everyone is unharmed."

Some people generously left another coin to help with barn expenses as they departed, as the party was clearly over.

Shame crashed over Ben, stronger than ever. And unable to hold himself up under the weight of such shame, he sank down onto a chair beneath a nearby tree and hid his head in his hands. He had done this. He'd started the fire that had almost killed not one but *two* of Ivette's sisters, not to mention their livestock.

He hated himself for allowing the first sip of ale. He clearly lost his self-control entirely under its influence, and now the Danvers sisters were paying for his mistakes.

You were never a good man, the voice inside his head taunted. His fears. His worries. His shame. He didn't remember much, but he knew he'd made far more mistakes than lighting a barn on fire.

Never again, he promised himself. *I will never drink again. Not even a sip.*

And he knew it was a promise he would keep. Because he never wanted to feel this way again, and he never wanted to cause others pain, especially not the people he cared about the most.

After the passing of many minutes, a soft pair of footsteps approached, but he couldn't bring himself to look at the sun. Not now when he was shrouded in so much darkness.

"I'm sorry," he cried. "I'm so sorry."

"Look at me," Ivette whispered.

He shook his head.

She gently grabbed hold of his chin and attempted to lift his gaze, but he pulled out of her grip.

"I didn't realize how liquor affected you," she murmured. "You've been avoiding it all this time, I've noticed that much, though I never understood why. I'm sorry I encouraged you. I didn't know."

"None of this is your fault." He stared off into the darkness, blinking back the heaviness in his eyes. "I am the one to blame." He paused, and still evading her gaze, he lied, "I have made other living arrangements."

"Ben, no. You can't leave."

But he only gestured to the burnt barn.

"Just stay here," she begged. "We'll figure this out. Together. I'm going to put Helen to bed, and I'll be right back."

She paused long enough to kiss his forehead before she disappeared, but the action only caused his shame to magnify. He didn't deserve her love. And he knew now that he never would. Especially not after what happened tonight.

First thing in the morning, he would leave Avorstead.

And he would never come back.

Chapter Ten

Ivette,

*   I am so ashamed of my behavior that I cannot face you. I suspected I may have had a problem with drinking in my past life, but tonight confirmed it. I vow to never drink another drop, but I know it's too late to fix what I have done. I hope one day you and your sisters will forgive me. In the meantime, I have found other living arrangements. I cannot burden you any longer.*

Ben

Ivette's hand flew to her mouth as she stared at the letter in her shaking fingers. Shock rooted her to the spot as she read the words again and again beneath the soft candlelight flickering from the table in her kitchen.

She could do nothing more than stare at the words, trying to make sense of the letter she had found on her doorstep, attempting to convince herself this was nothing more than a small hiccup in their relationship.

"What will we do?" Senna whispered so the others couldn't hear from the bedrooms. Because they all cared for him like family. She knew she wasn't the only one who loved him.

She wiped a stray tear away with her sleeve before slipping the letter into her pocket. "We give him some space. What happened was an accident. Surely, he will recognize as much and return to us soon."

Yet, she couldn't push away the pit in her stomach, the voice in her head that whispered she would never see him again. The thought of losing him entirely caused her heart to ache and her insides to twist uncomfortably. She loved him. And she would fight for him if necessary. But first he needed space and a clear head to think. Now was not the time to go after him, especially late at night in the darkness.

"Helen will be so upset," Senna murmured, swiping a hand across her running nose and tear-stained face.

"Things will turn out alright." She pulled her sister into an embrace even though she was the one who needed the comfort. She was immensely glad they'd gotten her sisters out before they were trapped in the flames. But still, it had been an accident.

Senna rubbed a hand across her back. "I know they will."

Ben squinted against the bright light filtering through the blanket over his head, groaning as he shifted onto his side on hard, scratchy wood. But then he recalled a few of the events from last night and groaned again, wishing he hadn't messed things up so soundly.

Most of the memories were a blur, likely things he'd said or small, inconsequential actions here and there. But the bigger things…

He'd come on too strong with Ivette.

And then the fire…

She'd been too forgiving after what had happened. She could have lost *two* sisters and a horse and a cow, just because he'd idiotically allowed himself to get drunk.

Never again, he vowed for the dozenth time in the past twelve hours as he pushed himself into a sitting position.

A blanket fell off him and into his lap, and he blinked back the bright light of late morning staring back at him from where he sat in Blain's wagon behind the mercantile. Good. No one had noticed his presence after he'd snuck into the wagon to sleep. Of course, it wasn't comfortable, but it was better than sleeping on the ground without something to protect him from the cold earth and chilly air.

He slipped off the wagon and winced when the jarring impact of his feet against the ground rattled the lingering ache in his head.

He smoothed his hair and clothing and started off down the road. Townsfolk greeted him with smiles and concern for the girls. But strangely enough, no one looked at him with disdain. Did they not know what happened? Who started the fire? His part in the unfortunate events the night prior?

Attempting to shrug it off, he focused on the one question probing at his mind. *What now?*

The coat containing his pocket watch and small number of coins remained at the Danvers home. Hiring a carriage was out of the question. Walking to Edilann could take a week, and he wasn't prepared for such a journey, nor did he think he would make it without passing out when the ache in his head festered with an unrelenting grip.

All he knew was he needed to leave Avorstead before he lost the will to do so entirely. Ivette deserved better than him.

A hand reached out blindingly fast from around the corner of a building and hooked onto his arm. Ben released a startled cry as a man pulled him into an alleyway and shoved him toward two other men, roughly his same age.

The air got knocked out of him as one of the men caught his stumbling self and pushed him toward the second man. They passed him back and forth like a ragdoll as he tried in vain to get his feet beneath him.

"Couldn't rid of us that easily!" one of them laughed.

Ben's heart leaped to his throat when he recognized the sheep rustler among them, and his pulse pounded through his veins as fear clutched onto him. What would they do to him? Injure him? Or worse?

Finally, he managed to find his feet long enough to pull his knife out of his boot. "Who are you?" he snarled, spinning to face each one to try to keep his knife between them.

"Whoa there." One of them held up a cautioning hand and stepped backward. "We're not trying to hurt you. We're only playing."

"So, it's true," another gasped in disbelief. "You *did* lose your memories."

"We thought you ran away to avoid getting married," said the third.

Ben spun to face the speaker, keeping the knife pointed toward him. "I won't ask again. Who are you?"

The man with his blond hair tied back gestured between all of them. "We're your friends." He pointed to each of them in tandem, himself first. "Tobie. Charles. Edward. Charles spotted you on the sheep farm and returned to Edilann to tell us. Of course, I didn't believe him. You've been gone so long, everyone thinks you're dead. Your mother has been out of sorts since your horse returned without you."

Edward, the dark-haired man, spoke behind him. "I think rather than reintroducing ourselves, you should tell him who *he* is. Because he clearly doesn't know."

The faintest look of concern crossed his blond friend's features before it was replaced by levity, treating this situation as if it were a joke. "You're Barnaby Allistair Mavis. And you are an Earl of Edilann."

He stared back at the three men, disbelief growing in his eyes by the second. No, no, no. This couldn't be true. He'd expected to come from a somewhat wealthy background. But an earl? To have an actual title?

"It's not true," he denied, shaking his head as his headache grew almost unbearable until the pounding pain threatened to collapse him. "There is no reason for me to be out in Leonia in such a case."

"Unless you were running away from marriage," Edward joked, flipping his dark, straight hair out of his eyes.

Tobie stroked his clean-shaven face, a thoughtful look in his eye. "True, feigning losing your memories and assuming a new identity is a bit much, even for you. What other reason did you have to come out here by yourself?"

"Loans?" Charles suggested, tucking his thumbs into a black belt.

His breath left his lungs as horror built up inside his chest, ready to explode. "Loans?"

Charles shrugged and ran a hand through his brown locks. "You took over for your father when he died a year ago. You know, John Mavis. Your father."

A pit of horror and disgust grew within his stomach until he nearly retched. Memory after memory flashed through his mind. Riding through a rainstorm in search of the Danvers family to acquire the debt they owed. His horse getting frightened by the thunder. The moments before the fall.

For years, the Danvers sisters had feared John Mavis coming after them. And he had. In the form of his son. For a debt that was not their fault, nor should have been put on their shoulders to begin with.

Ben, no *Barnaby*, collapsed to the ground when the pounding in his skull shook him relentlessly. He braced a hand against the dirt to keep himself upright, even as one of his friends held him aloft as he retched.

The memories crashed into him in a rush. He remembered when his father had died, how so much responsibility had been thrust upon his shoulders at once. How Barnaby turned to drinking to cope, only to be thrown into the pit of addiction, unable to stop himself from continuously having the poisonous substance in his body.

And then he remembered the king pressuring him to marry by his twenty-fourth birthday, lest the Edilann law come after him.

Mirabelle…

His fiancée came to mind with a rush of sickening guilt and self-hatred. Or rather, former betrothed, as another man had stolen her right from beneath his nose. Under the influence of the drink, he'd treated her terribly. Said things he regretted with his entire being. Made empty threats just to get her to comply when she rejected him again and again.

"No!" he sobbed, clawing at his head. "I don't want them. I don't want them!" But the memories kept flooding his mind. Every terrible thing he'd said. Every mean and spiteful thing he'd done. In the past several months, he'd tried his best to change. To become better. To give up the drink despite several relapses. But it wasn't enough. No amount of effort to be a good man would erase the black stains on his soul.

"Whoa there," Edward said again, and completely uncharacteristic of his friends, rather than mocking him for his tears, they comforted him. He patted Barnaby on the shoulder. "Let's get you home. You've been through…a lot."

"What about the girl?" Charles asked. "I saw you with her. She's clearly not one of your normal flings."

When Barnaby's only answer was to retch again, Edward and Charles lifted him to his feet on either side of him and helped him toward a black carriage waiting beneath the shadows of a tree.

Despite the ache in his head and the agony in his heart, he was grateful the townsfolk of Avorstead didn't have to witness the weakness of his body and mind. He didn't know what was going on with him. Perhaps his head hadn't fully recovered from the fall, and he needed more time to heal. Or maybe the aftereffects of the ale were still influencing the churning of his stomach and the spinning of his surroundings.

"I can't leave like this," he sobbed. "I can't just leave without…without…"

But he couldn't say goodbye. Because as he thought of Mirabelle and how he'd treated her, he wanted Ivette as far away from him as possible. He loved her with his entire being. And he knew putting distance between them was the best thing he could do for her.

His friends' voices became muffled through the turmoil pulsing through his ears as they helped him inside the carriage. One of them handed him a piece of parchment, a quill, and a bottle of ink.

He hastily scrawled the most heartbreaking message he'd ever written in his life.

Ivette –
I remember who I am. I am not a good man, and you deserve better.
Don't look for me.
I'm sorry.
– B

If anyone saw what he wrote, no one commented as Edward took the message from him, blotted the ink, folded the parchment into fourths, and dropped it off at the mercantile. Once everyone boarded the carriage, Charles tapped on the roof overhead, and the carriage jolted forward as the driver flicked the reins.

The rocking of the carriage caused his nausea to climb his throat. He placed his head between his knees and focused on breathing deeply through his nose and slowly out his mouth.

After several minutes, he lifted his head to glance out the window, only to find Avorstead a small dot against the ever-growing landscape. Falling from a cliff and bashing his head against a rock had changed his life forever, and although he was still close enough to see the town, ache festered in his chest as he already missed Ivette with his entire being.

But he had to let her go.

If she only knew the things he'd done in his past...

"Do you want an update on the happenings in your absence?" Charles asked.

No.

But as he glanced sideways at his friend, he realized why Charles had been there that day in the fields. His friends were...questionable influences. No one really knew what Charles actually did for a living, only that he claimed he worked as a trader for the king. He was a rather secretive man, but considering the terribly heartbreaking past Barnaby had unearthed years ago, one he kept secret to protect his friend, he didn't blame him. Either luck or fate had brought him all the way to Avorstead to accomplish his dirty work. Likely because no one could track him as easily in another kingdom.

"Yes," he whispered instead. His duties came before his personal needs. From now on.

"Well," Charles started, placing his hands behind his head and kicking his feet up on the seat in front of him, only for Edward to swat them back down. "You were missing for five days before your horse showed up without you. You dunce." He smacked Barnaby in the shoulder. "At least let *someone* know where you're going."

"I only went out for a ride," he protested.

Charles raised an eyebrow. "To Leonia? That's a far ride if you ask me."

Tobie leaned casually against the side of the carriage, fingers tapping against his knee as he continued where their friend left off. "Your mother sent dozens of soldiers to search for you. We can't send soldiers into Leonia, which is likely why we haven't found you until now."

Barnaby rested his head against the cool wall of the carriage and closed his eyes. A part of him wished Charles had never found him. Then he could have lived in blissful unawareness if his memories hadn't caught up to him.

But now?

Now he knew what a despicable man he was, and he lost the woman he loved.

His heart was broken beyond compare.

For most of the ride, he remained silent as he contemplated his life choices up to this point. Shirking off his duties as earl, finding solace in women and liquor, and filling his life with meaningless things that didn't make him happy. For several weeks, he'd caught a small taste of blissful happiness. No liquor. Just one woman. A family. Love. And he knew he didn't deserve it, but he wanted it.

As the sky darkened, they pulled off to the side of the road and entered a smooth clearing flat enough for the carriage to traverse. His friends started a fire and laid out bed rolls before passing around nuts, cheese, and bread.

Realizing he hadn't eaten all day, he consumed his meal quickly. And when Charles offered him mead, he declined with a shake of his head.

Next, he shucked off his shoes, and his feet breathed a sigh of relief at being unconfined within a pair of boots. He glanced up. Only to find all three men staring at him.

"What?" he grumbled, rubbing his temples in a circular motion. The headaches were improving since he'd recovered his memories, but they still managed to linger.

"What happened to you?" Tobie asked, rubbing a hand over his jaw.

"By all means," he gestured in the direction of Avorstead, "ask someone and they'll be able to recount the incident detail by detail. Nosy townsfolk."

But the other man shook his head. "You're eating like a starving pig. You've *never* refused liquor before. And you're awfully quiet, very unlike you."

Barnaby crossed his ankles and wrapped his arms around his knees, staring into the fire. He didn't answer their question when placing his feelings on display made him far too vulnerable for comfort.

Rather, he asked, "Has the king said anything? About me not being married?"

Edward snorted. "I think everyone's too worried about you being dead to care. But it sounds like you had a close call with death."

He ducked his head as his next question inspired more shame. "Does my mother know you found me?"

Tobie shook his head. "Only the three of us know. Didn't want to get hopes up just in case Charles was wrong."

A shiver shimmied down his spine, and he leaned closer to the fire for warmth. He was the second oldest in the group. Whereas Charles, the oldest at twenty-six, had the freedom to marry whenever he wished considering his wealthy but not titled background, the rest of them with titles or heirs to a title were counting down the days until they could put off marriage no longer.

"You can marry her," Edward said with a flip of his black hair. He lay on his bedroll, arms behind his head. "That girl. No law says you can't marry a peasant."

For several long moments, Barnaby stared into the flames, his eyes glistening when he already knew he couldn't for many reasons other than societal expectations.

"This has nothing to do with the law."

But rather a lot to do with his character and his past. Ivette deserved someone better.

The thought caused his pulse to pick up and his breathing to become ragged. His chest squeezed tight, and he focused on taking deep breaths to hide his distress from his friends. He managed to calm himself enough to lay on his bedroll. However, he didn't fall asleep quickly like he hoped he might. How could he? Especially when he recalled the feeling of Ivette in his arms. The sound of her laughter. The taste of her kiss.

Somehow, he awoke in the morning to one of his friends shoving him with their foot, followed by jesting and laughter. He managed to crack a smile for their benefit and kicked Tobie in the back of the knee. But otherwise for the rest of the journey to Edilann, he remained quiet and distanced from the others as he tried to plan rather than sulk.

All but one of his loan contracts were taken care of. Obviously, he couldn't allow the Danvers sisters to pay a single cent, especially after Ivette had saved his life. The loan was the first item of business upon his return.

He made a mental list of his tasks to complete by the week's end, and most of them required a lot of sucking up his pride and becoming a better man.

The carriage rolled over several bumps, bringing his attention to the changing scenery. Sparse farmland and buildings transitioned into a long road leading to a large estate. Despite learning to love a small town, the sight of his home brought a small measure of peace.

He could nearly smell the honey rolls wafting from the kitchen. The scent of a freshly manicured lawn. The tallow of dozens of candles lighting up the interior of the estate.

He gazed at the stone structure with a sense of awe and longing, growing bigger as the arching trees overhead abruptly cut off to reveal the circular drive with a large fountain spurting water directly from the center of the circle.

Servants waited in front of the doors as the carriage slowed, but before it rolled to a stop, Tobie burst out of the carriage and waved his arm like a lunatic. "We found him! We found him!"

Barnaby's jaw dropped as chaos ensued. Servants became frantic as they darted in and out of the estate. And when he stepped down from the carriage and onto gravel, the frantic hurry worsened.

He elbowed his friend in the ribs. Hard. "You just had to go and make this a big deal."

Tobie grinned. "It *is* a big deal. The lord has returned from a near death experience, mind you."

His only response was a scowl.

Before he managed to take a single step forward, his mother burst out of the front doors, dressed in a rumpled lavender gown. Her coiffed blonde hair was matted as if she hadn't bathed in days, and dark circles lay beneath her blue eyes.

"My baby," she gasped the moment their eyes locked. A sob escaped her as she picked up her skirts and rushed down the stairs. "My baby!"

He met her in a fierce embrace, not daring to ask her to refrain from calling him such silly, childish names when she sobbed into his shoulder. He wasn't sure who needed the comfort more—her or himself. But holding his mother after his world had been torn apart was exactly what he needed.

"I'll have the servants draw up a hot bath for you," his mother said while rubbing a hand soothingly across his back and wiping tears from her eyes.

"Thank you. I think I really need it."

Chapter Eleven

Yvette wiped the perspiration from her brow after throwing a bale of hay over the makeshift pen keeping the horse and cow quartered until they managed to build another barn. Of course, they hadn't the funds for such a project, especially after they'd paid half of their loan to one of the loaners. It was enough to satisfy the man. But he wanted the other half in one month's time.

She released a ragged breath as she rested her head against the scarred wood of the pen. It was clear now. She and her sisters would lose everything. The house. The property. The livestock. They would have nowhere to go. Nowhere to live. No way to support themselves.

Just one more month for her to figure out what to do.

All around her, life was falling apart. Even worse now that Ben had left for other *living arrangements*, and he hadn't bothered to visit for three days straight. Where was he? Who was he staying with? Why didn't he come home?

The note he'd left her crinkled in her pocket, and she pulled it out to read it for the hundredth time. She already knew it by heart, as it had been the words to cleave her soul in two.

"I've given you enough time and space," she huffed as she stuffed the parchment back into the pocket of her apron. "I don't know whether to berate or hug you, but I'm sure about to find out."

As she stomped toward the road, Senna fell into step beside her with a straw hat to shade her face from the sun. Unlike her, Senna was more prone to burning than to freckle.

"So, who's going to kick his behind?" her sister asked with a waggle of her brows. "You or I?"

Ivette smacked her arm at the suggestive tone in her voice. But then her lips twitched. "Obviously, it will be me."

Senna laughed and shoved her, and she shoved back. "Oh, he's in for it now!"

Ivette rolled her eyes as they continued toward the town. But as they entered the heart of Avorstead, townsfolk cast them pitying looks and whispered behind their backs, clearly talking about them.

Senna leaned closer. "What's going on? The barn incident wasn't *that* bad."

She frowned. "I don't know."

When they neared the mercantile, Blain's lips thinned as he followed their movement. Ivette's frown deepened as she tugged her sister in his direction and climbed the creaky wooden steps.

"What's going on?" she demanded, following him inside the store.

The man grimaced as he wiped his ink-stained hands on his dirtied apron. "He's gone. Three lads roughly his age sported him away several days ago. They left this behind, instructing me to give it to you when you next came by."

"Several days ago?" she said breathlessly. A pit of dread formed in her stomach as she hesitantly reached out for the folded parchment in Blain's hand and ventured outside onto the front porch of the mercantile with her sister following close behind. She slowly unfolded it and read the words written in Ben's own elegant script.

Ivette –
I remember who I am. I am not a good man, and you deserve better.
Don't look for me.
I'm sorry.
– B

"How could he possibly think this?" she gasped, the parchment rattling in her hands as hysteria grew within her. "He's a good man. I don't care what he's done in his past. Because he's a good man *now*."

A sob escaped, and then another, until fitful, weeping tears wracked her entire frame. She sank onto the top step of the porch and cried as her sister held her close, patting her back and whispering soothing things into her ear.

"How could he leave me like this?" she cried, wiping tear after tear with her apron. "He couldn't bother to bid me farewell in person? Did I mean nothing to him?"

"Stop," Senna chided, now wiping the tears with her own skirts. "No man looks at a woman like he looked at you if you meant nothing to him."

"But…but…but…" Another wave of heartache crashed into her as she continued sobbing, unable to help the tears despite the looks she received from passing townsfolk. "I told him I loved him. And…and…and he didn't say it back. I must be a fool to have fallen for him so hard."

Her sister gripped her on either side of her face and looked at her with a stern expression. "That man loved you. I know it. Surely, he must have a good reason to leave like this." More tear wiping. "It sounds like his friends came for him. Or brothers. Remember how he lost his memories in the first place?"

She nodded, remembering the vast amounts of blood, the days of unconsciousness, the fight for his life.

Continuing, Senna said, "I can't imagine getting them *back* was any easy feat either. He must be disoriented. Perhaps hurting and scared."

"He'd been suffering a headache for days," Ivette admitted as she remembered him being unable to enjoy the party. At least before the ale. Although he'd admitted complete fault for his actions, she couldn't help but take some of the blame for offering the ale to him in the first place. She should have known…

"I know it's trivial compared to all our other problems." She hiccupped and swiped at her tears, but they kept coming.

"It's not trivial," Senna soothed. "You love him. We all could see it. It's why we stepped back." She squeezed Ivette's knee. "Because the connection you two shared was truly something special, and we didn't want to jeopardize it by fighting over the same man."

"But he's gone now," she cried into her lap, unable to stop the relentless sobs from escaping all over again. "I don't even know his name."

Senna rubbed her back and kissed the top of her head. "He'll return to us." A wagon passed and kicked up dirt, cutting into her hysterics. "Somehow, I know it to be true."

"All of it."

The head maid's jaw gaped as she stared back at him. "All of it? But Your Lordship—"

"All of it," Barnaby emphasized again, gesturing to the crates of liquor stored in a corner of the kitchen and the full shelves. "I want all of it gone. Sell it. Destroy it if you must. You can cook with wine, but there will be no more mead, ale, beer, nothing at all in this household." He grimaced at how callous, and perhaps unfair, it sounded. "Personal stashes may remain. Nothing more."

At least until he had more of a handle on his current state of addiction. Yes, he still vowed to never drink again. But someday, perhaps he might be able to serve it to guests on special occasions.

Until then…

"I want it gone by the week's end," he stressed, followed by a quiet word of thanks to the baffled servants.

"Your Lordship." The head butler bowed at the waist as he entered the kitchens and held out a silver platter ladled with business and correspondence. It had been a nightmare to catch up on all of it in his absence, but he couldn't seem to catch a break either.

A letter with the royal seal lay on top of the pile, and his blood ran cold. He scooped up the letters and ambled out of the room, using the knife in his pocket to slide beneath the seal. The letter unfurled, detailing the royal family's well wishes over his health after what had transpired and an invitation to him and his mother for tea in a couple weeks. It briefly mentioned marriage with a veiled warning sweetened by words of flattery.

If he didn't marry soon, he would face bigger problems than a simple slap on the wrist.

He sighed and rubbed his temples. Since leaving Ivette, he found it difficult to focus on anything, to find the drive to wake up each morning, to function at all. The thought of her festered in every corner of his heart and mind.

He missed her. And he didn't want to marry any other woman but her.

But he must.

The women in his circle were bred for this life. No one would bat an eye to have a husband who didn't love them. But Ivette…she deserved far better, even if he loved her with his entire heart.

Someone touched his elbow, and he nearly jumped out of his skin, only to find his mother staring at him with a concerned expression.

"I called you from down the hallway," she said.

His gaze traveled down the rug-lined corridor with natural light pooling in from the oval-cut windows. Filmy white drapes lay secured on either side of the windows with red tassels adding a drop of color to the space.

Today, his mother looked far more refreshed than days earlier. She wore a bold blue gown, her hair no longer matted against her head. She'd birthed him young, so she still possessed a youthful glow in her early forties.

"I have a lot on my mind."

Her expression softened as she cupped his cheek. "You've been doing so much good for the people of Edilann. I've seen how hard you've been working to correct your father's...mistakes." She dropped her hand and lowered her gaze. "I was so afraid you would end up like him. I'm glad to see I'm wrong."

Barnaby frowned at only recently realizing the wrongs his father had committed. All his life, he'd looked up to him. But now? It was difficult to forge his own path.

"You've been distant and quiet ever since you returned," his mother said, drawing his attention back to her. "What's weighing on your mind?"

The thought of Ivette crashed into his soul, shattering it like shards of glass lying at his feet. For a moment, he debated remaining silent. But this was his *mother*. He trusted her.

"I met someone."

"That's a good thing!" she exclaimed, but when he didn't smile, her demeanor fell with it. "Why aren't you happy?"

"She's... She lives on a sheep farm. She's not...upper class. And...and I think she deserves better than me."

She smiled reassuringly as she patted his arm. "Don't worry about what others think. If she makes you happy..."

"It doesn't change the fact that I was more like Father than I knew." He hung his head. "I've made too many mistakes. She doesn't know who I am, and I want to keep it that way."

He pushed through the layers of heartache and dejection to force out his next words. "The king has made it clear I cannot wait any longer. I need to marry. Perhaps an engagement for now will suffice." He ignored the heartbreak reflecting back on his mother's face as he continued. "I thought hosting a ball would be the next course of action. You know, having all the eligible women in one place rather than me having to make dreary appointment after dreary appointment to home after home."

"This is no trivial matter, Barnaby. You can't just pick your future wife out of a crowd like the choice is inconsequential."

"It doesn't matter anymore," he said quietly. After Ivette... He could never love another. And therefore, a wife was just a wife if he denied himself the woman he loved.

Finally, his mother nodded. "I will see to the arrangements. The Mother Goddess knows you could never pull off such a feat."

He only smiled, though he was sure it didn't reach his eyes. If only she knew...

After giving her cheek a kiss, he continued on his way to the exit of the estate when his surroundings spun with a sudden heave. His chest ached. The breaths from his lungs escaped as rapid bursts.

He ducked into a nearby empty room to avoid notice.

The agony in his chest knocked the air out of his lungs. Ragged breaths escaped him. The world spun around him. He clutched the fabric of his shirt over his heart when the painful throb became too much to bear. With his other hand, he braced himself against the back of a chair.

Shaky exhales accompanied the feeling of panic as he thought of Ivette. He loved her so much, it literally hurt to be apart from her.

He knew it sounded extreme. But he could not live without her. He could not possibly survive a marriage to another woman. But he had to try.

After his breathing calmed a fraction, he felt another presence and turned his head, only to find his mother watching him from around the corner with a pinched mouth and worried eyes.

Swallowing the pit in his throat, he turned on his heel and exited the door.

He would survive this. He *would*.

A new sort of trepidation pressed on his shoulders as he stepped into the carriage waiting outside. It jolted forward, and he tried his best to remain stoic as he stared at the empty, velvety cushioned seats in front of him.

He'd committed many wrongs in his past, and perhaps this was one of his biggest mistakes. He owed it to Mirabelle to make this right.

But as the dirt roads transitioned into cobblestone streets, his hands perspired, and his leg bounced up and down. The inner city of Edilann lay sprawled around him, and his carriage gathered plenty of watchful stares as they passed carts, wagons, and people on the streets.

Edilann was divided into sections. The palace towered above the large city. Most of the businesses resided in the eastern section while on the opposite side of the city lay numerous residential homes. The wealthy owned their own homes and land while most others lived in buildings closer together. A smaller section of homes belonged to people the king owned. Scribes, soldiers, servants, and to his unfortunate dismay, personal bodyguards. Or in simpler terms, Prince Sterling's personal bodyguard. Mirabelle's husband, Gilberd Keats.

The carriage pulled up to a property with a small yard and house. A box of flowers rested beneath one of the windows, bringing a pop of color to the faded brown exterior of the home.

He frowned when he spotted the boots resting outside the front door on the porch, and his frown deepened as he exited the carriage only to find a horse grazing in the small pasture to the side.

"Argh," he muttered. "That big oaf is here?" He heaved a long sigh and slapped his driver on the shoulder. "I think I'm about to get my arse handed to me. If I don't make it, tell my mother I love her."

The driver cracked a small grin. "It's good to see your humor returned. I will only intervene if necessary, milord."

As if summoned, the man in question opened the door and slammed it shut, a scowl on his face. He stood a lot taller than Barnaby, his muscles twice the size of his as well.

"What the hell do you think you're doing here?" Gilberd asked, pushing his sleeves up to his elbows as he tromped toward him. "I thought we settled this with your last black eye. Did you come back for more?"

Barnaby held up his hands in a display of peace—but mostly to protect his face. He *did* have a ball coming up after all, and he didn't want to sport a black eye or two for the event.

"I came to talk to Mirabelle."

Gilberd scoffed and spat into the dirt.

The petite woman slipped outside and stood at the top steps of the porch, dark brown hair pulled back in a bun, a hand on her hip, bringing attention to her…

"Oh…" He mimicked her stance and planted his fists on his hips. "When did that happen?" He gestured to her round belly, ready to pop any day.

But Gilberd roughly grabbed him by the front of the shirt and shoved him backward. He barely managed to stay on his feet. "Get off our property, Barn-yard. Now."

"I swear, I only need one minute of her time. No more. And then I promise to never return."

"Gil," Mirabelle murmured, waddling down the porch steps toward them. She placed a hand on her husband's arm, which seemed to ease the man's agitation. They exchanged no words but spoke with their gazes alone.

Gilberd sighed and crossed his arms over his chest. "Fifty more seconds and counting."

Barnaby shifted his gaze to his former betrothed, and the same shame that had been haunting him for months attacked him all over again. She was a beautiful woman, yes, which had gotten him into trouble in the first place. But he'd never loved her, and he was immensely glad she'd found Gilberd instead.

"I have discovered that I am…not myself when under the influence of the drink," he started slowly, perspiration trickling down the back of his neck when he was overly aware of Gilberd's cutting gaze on him. "I did and said many things I regret. Things that hurt you. And I am immensely sorry. I know I don't deserve it, but I hope someday you might forgive me."

Mirabelle raised an eyebrow and glanced over his shoulder toward his driver. As if not wanting him to overhear, she lowered her voice. "You told me you planned to pass me *discreetly* around the upper class for favors after you *had your fun* with me."

Ah, yes. The shame. It smashed into him at full force. His head nearly lowered at the guilt of his words, but he forced himself to hold her gaze. "It was an empty threat, something the liquor convinced me was a funny thing to say at the time. It was not funny. At all." He released a long breath and trekked through the mud of his mistakes. "Edilann law dictates I must marry by the time I turn twenty-four. You were by far the prettiest unmarried woman of my acquaintance at the time." He swallowed. "I mucked things up badly."

"Ten more seconds, Barn-a-breath," Gilberd growled.

"I've been sober for over a month now," *not counting the relapse in Avorstead...* "and my head is clearer than it's ever been. I deeply regret what happened between us. The things I said. Trapping you into a betrothal with your debt. Making a fool of you." He spoke quickly now, sure his sixty seconds were up entirely. "I am glad you found Gilberd. I want to see you happy."

Her guarded expression fell. Her hands previously resting on her hips now rested over her belly. "You've had months to apologize. Why now?"

A tortured expression took hold of his face and refused to let go. "I want to be a good man."

He didn't elaborate.

But she seemed to see through him. "You met someone, didn't you?"

"I want her to be happy, too. So, I let her go."

Mirabelle shocked him by grabbing onto his arm as he turned to leave. "You've come a long way since we first met." She gave him a gentle squeeze. "Perhaps you deserve happiness as well."

"I deserve nothing." He pulled out of her grip and nodded to both of them. "Perhaps I'll see you again, Gil-brat, at the next ball. Standing still with nothing to do but look bored out of your mind as you guard the prince."

The other man scoffed. "Better than prancing around like a donkey." Gilberd kept his hand by his side, out of Mirabelle's sight, as he flipped him the bird.

Barnaby laughed as he climbed into the carriage and slammed the door closed behind him. Some things never changed.

And he sort of preferred it that way.

Chapter Twelve

One of the worst things to endure was watching as one's children suffered.

Eloise Mavis stood at the window of the drawing room long after Barnaby's carriage rolled away. The filmy white drapes fluttered in the breeze entering through the panes. A peaceful afternoon stared back at her with blue skies and a promise of sunshine.

Yet, the turmoil in her heart far outmatched the serene atmosphere outside.

When the soldiers at her beck and call hadn't been able to find Barnaby, she'd convinced herself he was dead. And now?

A mother knew their offspring like the back of their hand. And her boy was hurting because he loved a woman.

Had she rejected him? Was that it?

Slowly, she shook her head and clasped her fingers in front of her. He'd indicated he didn't feel worthy of the woman.

Perhaps she had no say in how he felt about himself, but she was still the woman of the house. She had the power to make things happen.

Her eyes sparked with determination as she located the head maid in the kitchen still fumbling as she and the other servants carried out Barnaby's task. She pulled the frazzled woman aside.

"In two weeks' time, we will hold a ball."

The maid dipped her head respectfully. "What will we have on the menu?"

Eloise's mouth twitched as she watched the rest of the servants for their reaction as she answered. "We will need to stretch the budget. No formal dinner this time. But we will have plenty of refreshments." She nearly cracked a smile as excitement alighted within her. "We will invite the nobility of our acquaintance…and extend the invitation to the commoners as well."

A silver platter clattered to the floor behind the island table, and a maid stared at her with wide, disbelieving eyes.

"The c-c-commoners?" the head maid stuttered. "We have never done such a thing."

"Then now is the time to start a new tradition." She turned her back and finally allowed her smile to surface. "We have a sheep girl to catch."

With a swish of her skirts, she exited the kitchens. When she stood at the bottom of the staircase with a plush red carpet lining rich, mahogany wood, she glanced both ways to ensure no one noticed her as she began her climb to the second floor, her hand draped lightly over the banister railing. Every part of her urged her to run, to conclude her snooping before Barnaby returned. But a lady never ran—she floated.

Therefore, she floated across the next landing on silent, nimble feet, her slippers making nary a sound, until she stood in front of her son's bedroom door.

She never dared to venture this way, afraid of what she might find. Or hear. But her snooping mattered more than ever today, and she swore to see it through.

She reached for the door handle and turned, only for it to resist her efforts.

Locked.

Placing her hands on her hips, she took a step back and frowned.

Her late husband, John, had always kept a spare key on the top of the door frame. Especially because he'd gotten drunk often and formed a habit of losing his keys.

She stood on the tips of her toes, struggling to reach the top of the wood. But then her finger brushed against something cold, knocking a single key onto the carpet with a soft *thud*.

"Gotcha!" she whispered triumphantly as she scooped the key up and fit it inside the lock. She turned the handle, and the door opened without resistance.

The interior of Barnaby's room matched his neat appearance. Nothing out of place. Everything organized in an orderly fashion. Books lay in neat rows in the bookcase. Stacks of paper rested in perfect piles on his desk. The outfit he likely planned to wear tomorrow lay folded on the bedroom bench in tidy rows with his shoes resting on the floor at the bench's base.

Glancing back at the door open a crack to make sure she was alone, she approached the desk first and thumbed through the documents and correspondence lying on top.

When she failed to find what she was looking for, she opened drawer after drawer, sifting through his belongings while trying to bat away the guilt eating at her conscience.

"This is in your best interest," she murmured to herself as she moved to the bedside tables next. The table on the left side of the bed lay empty. But the right…

She hastily snatched the pieces of folded parchment from the drawer and unfolded them one at a time. Each was addressed to a man named Ben. But at the bottom…

Always, Ivette

"Ivette!" she exclaimed triumphantly, reading the top letter once again just to make sure. They were obviously love letters, and the content reassured her that they were written during his absence from Edilann. The woman's name was unique, giving her hope to find her easily. In the instance that the search proved difficult, she counted on the upcoming ball to draw the woman out.

If it was the last thing she ever did, she would see Ivette married to her son.

She memorized the name by heart before placing the letters back carefully to prevent Barnaby from learning of her snooping.

With a large smile on her face, she exited his room. And locked the door behind her.

It rained. Again.

Gray storm clouds relentlessly poured their tears down from the heavens, matching the way Ivette's soul wanted to weep—how it had already wept until nothing remained but achy numbness.

She knew it was silly—crying over a man. Her heart had endured tougher times than this. But this time, the loss was too much to bear. Or perhaps, she could not stand to lose any more, and the final loss—losing Ben—managed to break her entirely.

Her boots slipped through the mud as she struggled to keep her feet beneath her on the path from the cow pen to the house. Milk slopped out of the pail she held with each slick step. Rain drenched her clothing, and her hair clung to her forehead and face. Although her body wanted to collapse from sheer physical and emotional exhaustion, she kept going. For her sisters. Because they needed her to be strong.

Thunder rolled across the sky, reminding her of the fateful night Ben had fallen from the cliffside. Lightning lit up the hill, and her gaze traveled across the expansive fields to the tree where Ben had kissed her.

So much emotion had claimed each of his kisses, his gentle touches, the sweet whispers from his lips. He'd never said he returned her feelings, but she felt it in her heart that he did.

Whatever you did in your past, it doesn't matter, she internally said.

Another voice spoke in the faintest whisper, nearly too quiet to discern over the rumbling thunder and pattering rain. *You can go after him.*

To where? Edilann? And then what?

She huffed as she envisioned the conversations she'd have with strangers about trying to find a man named Ben who didn't actually exist. She had no leads except Edilann.

And Edilann was a sizeable kingdom.

She swiped the large sleeve of Ben's coat across her cheek, which only inspired more tears when she caught his scent beneath her nose. She had no business wearing his coat. But it was big and warm, and it smelled like him.

The door creaked as she pulled it open, only managing to spill more of the milk on the front porch step. As she entered, her sisters hushed where they all sat around the table. Senna held a document in her hands, her eyes wide as she stared back at her.

"Ivette," Senna breathed, pushing the stack of documents toward her.

"No." She quickly turned away to hide her quivering chin as she set the pail of milk on the counter. "I can't handle any more letters or notes." Her fingers trembled as she covered her eyes with her sleeve. "No more."

"I promise," Lily said, pushing the documents closer. "You will want to see this."

Steeling herself for the worst of news, she slowly turned and picked up the stack of parchment, dread filling every pore in her body as she read the first line.

I, John Mavis, extend the loan amount of—

Ivette dropped the loan documents to the table and covered her face in her hand. "They found us," she lamented with a sob. "We'll end up in prison or worse. We have to flee. We have to—"

"Read it again," Senna urged, this time pointing to a scrawl of black ink at the top of the page.

PAID IN FULL

"What?" she exclaimed, snatching the documents again. She flipped through page after page, realizing they were a copy of the original loan documents given to her father, now under her care.

On the last page, the entire loan amount was struck out, again saying *PAID IN FULL* and signed in elegant scrawl, a name she didn't recognize but a surname that she did.

Barnaby Allistair Mavis.

Senna released a joyous laugh as she next shoved a letter into her hands. Ivette's eyes flew across the page, the shock filling her more and more with each word.

To Vivian Danvers, or who this may concern,

The loan taken out under Vivian Danvers has been paid in full. No more is owed. The donor overpaid as well, sending along the rest within the envelope. No more action is required at this time.

Lord Barnaby Allistair Mavis

"Could it have been Father?" Lily breathed.

Too stunned to speak, Ivette collapsed onto a chair as she stared at the documents before her. Just like that, a huge burden had been lifted from her shoulders.

Senna answered for her. "Father would never have done such a thing. He abandoned us. And unless he suddenly grew a conscience…"

Ivette's body unfroze enough to reach inside the envelope lying on the table for a velvety leather pouch filled with coins, and the breath got knocked from her lungs all over again. It was enough to pay off the second loan. All of it. Plus some.

"This can't be real," she finally said in a gaspy breath, counting out the coins a second time just to be certain. "Father would have gloated if it had been him. Very few people know about the loans to begin with, and I know for a fact no one in this town has enough to pay off so much money."

"What about Ben?" Grace ventured.

The entire room fell silent. The shock of her words grabbed onto her ankles and climbed her body like vines. The timing of the loans being paid off was too coincidental. And they had all speculated that Ben likely was filthy rich according to his state of dress.

"No..." She shook her head in denial. "Surely, he wouldn't have bothered." Especially after the way he'd left.

Each one of them gave her a pointed look filled with disbelief. The truth of the situation slowly dawned on her. Ben had helped them pay off the first half of the second loan. And then they had mentioned the name of the first loaner. Once he'd regained his memories, it likely hadn't been hard to find John Mavis's heir in Edilann.

"Mercy!" she gasped as she launched to her feet and sprinted down the hallway to her room. She shoved the door open and began hastily throwing clothing and essentials into a bag. If she moved quickly, she might be able to catch the next wagon out of town.

Of course, her sisters followed. Siblings were nosey, after all.

"Where are you going?" Senna asked from where she sat at the foot of her own bed. But the sly, knowing smile on her face gave her away.

"I'm going to find Ben." She tossed a hairbrush into the bag, followed by a spare pair of slippers just in case. She couldn't help herself as she also included the letters Ben had written her. "I don't care if he told me not to find him. I'm not going to give up on him."

Her sisters squealed, Lily and Helen holding hands and jumping up and down in a circle on the rug. Ben was family. And no matter what her future ended up looking like, she swore to bring him back home.

With her bag packed, she hastily tied her boots and threw a cloak over her shoulders over Ben's coat. A metal jangle grabbed her attention with the movement, and with a start, she reached into one of the pockets and pulled out his pocket watch.

It dangled from a golden chain, the smooth metal catching on the light filtering through the window. Although the pocket watch wasn't much to go off of, she could take it to a jeweler and try to find out where it was made.

Tucking the watch into her own pocket, she next snatched the loan papers from the table and turned them every which way, next surveying the envelope they had come in.

"There is no return address," she remarked.

Lily answered. "A man came by in his carriage. I asked him his name but all he mentioned was he worked for Lord Mavis."

She decided against bringing the documents and instead slipped Lord Mavis's letter inside her bag. Perhaps it would prove useful for later. "Senna, can you handle paying the loaner the rest of the money?"

Her sister nodded. "I'll take care of everything in your absence."

"I could be gone for weeks," she warned.

Rather than protesting, her sisters pushed her toward the door. "Go find him!" Lily called with a giggle. "And if you marry the bloke, don't forget about us."

Ivette laughed and pulled each one of them into an embrace, and before she managed to choke on her emotions, she burst outside, only to find that the patter of rain had died down, and patches of blue in the sky promised sunshine in the near future.

She started toward the road, only to pause when she noticed one of the sheep moving its mouth in agitation. As if instead of grass, it had found a stick and struggled to expel it.

She approached to help the poor creature when something small fell from the sheep's teeth and plopped onto the grass. Confusion pulled at her brows as she stooped to pick up the item, only to inhale sharply when she found a thick gold ring with a red gemstone inlaid in the precious metal.

The ring was large enough to belong to a man.

Ben...

She recalled the finger he'd shown her with an indent in his skin. A finger he was sure he'd worn a ring on.

It had to belong to him.

Placing it in her pocket next to the watch, she strode toward the road with determined steps. The man didn't want to be found. But he was about to learn just how persevering and dedicated she could be.

Chapter Thirteen

"What is this?" Barnaby furiously strode into the drawing room and waved an invitation in the air. "Every eligible maiden in the kingdom? Hmm?"

But his mother only smiled as she daintily set her teacup on its saucer with the faintest *plink*. "I thought you would approve."

"How is this approval?" He slapped the paper onto the table in front of her, the movement rattling the porcelain. "I said a ball. Not a never-ending fray of tittering females."

Her smile turned sly. "If you are to pick your bride out from a crowd with hardly a thought, why does it matter anyway?"

He plopped into a cushioned chair and slouched with his legs outstretched. He leaned his head back against the chair, covered his face with his hands, and groaned. "I will become the laughingstock of the entire kingdom. You do realize I will never live this down."

"Nonsense." She waved away the notion with a gloved hand. "I've already received responses from dozens of upper-class families as well as many from lower classes. The ball is all anyone can talk about."

"I noticed," he muttered. "My friends have been ribbing me nonstop all day."

"And…" She stared at the teacup, but he felt her attention on him, nonetheless. "You are a very sought-after man in the marriage market. Many women want a chance to catch your eye."

"I'm sure," he scoffed. "Especially after what happened with my last failed engagement."

His mother reached across the table and patted him sympathetically on the knee. "It's never too late for second chances. It will go right this time around. I'm sure of it."

The heartache lying in wait around every corner of his mind returned with a vengeance as he thought of Ivette. He rubbed a hand over the ache in his chest in an attempt to massage the pain from his body. But it lingered.

He immediately dropped his hand when he caught his mother watching.

"One more week," she said in a cautious tone, still watching him carefully. "Are you ready?"

"No." He unfolded himself from the chair and stalked out of the room, but not before kicking the door frame with his shoe over his frustration at himself.

"Love you!" his mother called after him.

"Love you, too," he grumbled before exiting the room and walking briskly across the hallway, down a set of stone steps leading to the lower levels of the estate, and toward the armory. Nothing eased his frustration more than spending some quality time with his large collection of knives and daggers. He only had to fight the temptation to storm outside to the stables, mount his horse, and gallop all the way to Avorstead to the woman his heart wanted more than anything in the kingdom.

The feat seemed nearly impossible.

Keys jangled in his hand as he pulled them out of his pocket when he reached the wood and metal door at the end of a dark, chilly hallway with stone floors, walls, and ceilings. He fit the key inside the lock, but paused when the turn met no resistance.

In a quick movement, he threw open the door and reached for the dagger tied to his belt. Only to freeze when he found his friend lounging on a bench, reading a book.

"Tobie!" he gasped with exasperation as he shoved the door closed behind him. "Nearly gave me a start. How did you get in?"

His friend jangled a key in front of his face, and when Barnaby made a grab for it, the other man stuffed it down his breeches. He smacked the book out of Tobie's hands, and it slapped onto the floor.

His friend scowled. "I was reading that."

"And now you aren't."

He and Tobie had been friends since they were children, as their mothers were friends as well. He was like a brother who came and went as he pleased whether or not Barnaby was home.

"Thought I'd find you here." Tobie's shoulder-length blond hair fell over his face without its tie as he sat up before running his fingers through the strands. "You usually come here to mope."

"I'm not moping." But the bite was missing from his tone, and instead his words came out as a somber sigh. He crossed the room to his ornate collection of daggers from across the nine kingdoms. Some with jewel-encrusted hilts with shining gems of green, blue, red, and yellow. Others with engraved wooden and metal hilts. He enjoyed cleaning the decorative weapons far too much just to watch them shine. But today, he passed over them completely in favor of his throwing knives.

He unlocked a glass case and pulled out a bundled wrap, setting it on a nearby table. He shrugged out of his vest and unfastened the first two buttons of his white shirt beneath to give him more mobility. Next, he unraveled the bundle of cloth, revealing each of his knives lying in a neat row and sharpened to perfection.

For a moment, he stared at the knives, recalling the game he'd won in Avorstead in the name of a beautiful woman named Ivette Danvers.

But then he recalled the way he'd come onto her after his ale incident. The barn burning. Helen crying.

He picked up the first knife and threw it with deadly accuracy across the room. The tip embedded directly in the middle of one of the circular targets with more gauges in the wood than he could count.

"You're right," Tobie commented. "You're not moping. That's anger I sense."

"I keep making mistakes," he growled, mostly at himself.

He threw another knife into the next target. It also hit the middle ring.

"And you're about to make another one." Tobie bent to retrieve his book from the ground, opening the pages but not reading it. "This ball is a terrible idea."

"And I suppose you have a better one? I'm out of time."

Tobie leaned forward on his knees and leafed through the book as Barnaby picked up the next knife, testing the balance in his hand. It was perfectly balanced. Perfectly sharp.

His friend shrugged and grinned. "Ask the king for more time? While you're at it, ask on my behalf as well."

Barnaby snorted as he lifted the knife with perfect poise and concentration. As heir to a barony, Tobie was next in line for marriage with no serious prospects. But at least he still had time to sort things out.

"Marry the sheep girl," Tobie said at the same time he threw the knife. It arced through the air, spinning twice before slicing the target on the edge ring, ripping through the corner, and clattering against the stone wall behind it.

He stared at the knife for far too long, the ache in his heart returning to match the heavy, labored breaths in his lungs.

"I cannot."

Barnaby had made too many mistakes in his life, especially in the past year. Ivette would realize soon enough that her life would be better without him in it. Even if he was the one who had to sacrifice his own happiness to make it happen.

Ivette slumped exhaustedly into the passenger wagon after her fourth failed attempt to locate the origin of the watch. Only one of the jewelers had said Lord Mavis lived somewhere in the bigger city of Edilann, which would be her next course of action in tracking down Ben. But otherwise…

She found no such luck.

Pulling out the pocket watch, she ran a thumb over the smooth, gold metal just as the wagon lurched forward. She traced Ben's initials with her finger, feeling each groove inlaid in the metal.

B.A.M.

Minutes passed of frustrating puzzlement, and she tore her attention away from the watch to relieve the strain in her eyes. Flickering shadows passed over the wagon as they passed beneath a canopy of trees. Sparkling water reflected the sun's light to her right. The horse's hooves clomped ahead, giving her a steady rhythm to focus on rather than the despondent melody in her heart.

She refused to give up, and she reminded herself that every turn of the wagon's wheel brought her closer and closer to Edilann's capital city. But Edilann was a large kingdom, and Ben could be anywhere in one of the six provinces.

Which was why she decided to begin her search anew in the big city and work her way outwards from there.

Tension strung her muscles tight around her shoulders, and she closed her eyes for a few moments to massage the strain. After six days of traveling and questioning and searching, her body desperately begged for a good night's rest.

The wagon rolled to a stop, followed by the snort of one of the horses hitched to the conveyance. Ivette watched as a small group climbed the steps of the wagon and settled onto one of the long benches on either side. A group of ladies sat closest to her, each wearing Edilann's style of dress with corsets tied over loose blouses and roomy skirts in a variety of shades and patterns.

One of the women cooled herself with a red fan, and only when the wagon started up again did she turn to her neighbor and continue the conversation they'd cut off earlier.

"He's inviting all the eligible maidens in the kingdom," the woman wearing a blue bonnet gossiped with her nose turned up in a snobbish manner. "If that doesn't reek of desperation, I don't know what does."

One of the others wearing a plaid, yellow skirt lifted an eyebrow. "Have you *seen* the man? He could have any woman he wants with the snap of his fingers." She shook her head. "No, no, no. I think he's looking for someone. Why else would he extend the invitation to *everyone?*"

"Who could he *possibly* be looking for? Likely, the woman would be wrapped around his little finger already."

"Perhaps me?" The woman with the fan flared it flirtatiously in front of her face while batting her eyelashes. "If I have the chance to turn the lord's head, I sure am gonna take it."

"As if Barnaby would ever look in *our* direction," she scoffed. "He's got women in jewels and fine gowns at his fingertips, and even more that will show up at his ball tomorrow night."

Ivette perked up at the mention of Barnaby. She dared to cut into their conversation, the snobbish woman looking annoyed while the others seemed excited to share in their gossip. "Barnaby Mavis?"

"Yes," Yellow Skirt sighed dreamily. "He's the most exquisite gem to walk Edilann."

A man sitting beside her coughed and glared momentarily before shifting in his seat, angled away from her as he read the periodical in his hands.

"I am actually looking for Lord Mavis." She pulled out the pocket watch and showed it to the others, realizing her mistake too late that someone might target her to steal it if she wasn't careful. But the damage was already done. "I think he can lead me to the man who owns this."

"Huh…" Red Fan took the watch from her and inspected it close to her face as if she couldn't see far. "A lot of wealthy men carry such personal items. Likely a family heirloom of some sort."

Desperation led her actions as she scrambled for the ring in her pocket next and held it out as well. "And what of this?"

All three women gasped at once, enough to draw the man's attention from his periodical. He choked on his spittle, his face turning red as he pointed to the small piece of jewelry. "Where did you get that?"

"It belongs to my…friend."

Before she could stop him, the man grabbed the ring from her and inspected it between pinched fingers. "There's no mistaking it," he murmured. "This was cut from the Edilann ruby."

Ivette quickly snatched it back and pocketed it before it could disappear again. "What does that mean?"

"It means," said Snobby Blue Bonnet, "that the king extended it personally to the wearer, or rather the wearer's predecessors. What you are looking at is the ring belonging to an earl."

"Or baron," Yellow Skirt cut in.

But Ivette hardly discerned the words when blood pulsed loudly through her ears as shock climbed her body and settled as ice in her chest. She grabbed the pocket watch back from the woman and flipped it over to reveal the initials engraved into the metal.

B.A.M.

Barnaby Allistair Mavis.

"Mercy!"

Her frantic fingers dug through her bag until they closed around the letter from Lord Mavis. Next, she smoothed out a letter from Ben on her lap until the two letters rested side by side.

Every slant and swoop in the lettering was identical, down to the elegant loop of the "B" in his name. The sudden realization knocked the air from her lungs, and she struggled to breathe as she leaned back against the bench. Her Ben was Lord Barnaby Allistair Mavis.

Then what did that mean, exactly?

Surely, the only reason Ben—err, Barnaby—had been on their property those months ago was to collect the loan that was due. But he'd fallen and hit his head, forgetting his mission and his past. He'd helped them pay off half their loan. And then after he'd left, he'd paid off the other half and pardoned them for the loan in their mother's name.

"And you say you're not a good man," she murmured to herself as she pressed both letters to her heart and fought back a wave of tearful gratitude.

Never in her life had she expected to fall in love with an *earl*. And a part of her whispered she would never have a chance with him, considering her lowly station and his high rank in society. She hoped more than anything he would consider her.

But if he didn't…the least she could do was express her gratitude for what he'd done for her family. Pulling them entirely out of debt and taking the heavy burden from their shoulders was not something she could brush aside.

Why? she couldn't help but ask herself. Why had he done it?

You know why.

She closed her eyes as she recalled his bright smile, the beautiful blue of his eyes, the blond sweep of his hair. High cheekbones. Strong jaw. Soft lips…

The way he'd held her tenderly in his arms. How he'd kissed her with sweet intent. The soft murmurings of his gentle voice.

Yes, yes, she knew she sounded like a lovestruck, giggling female like the others in the wagon, but it wasn't just a fancy for her.

"He's the most exquisite gem to walk Edilann."

Oh, she certainly didn't doubt it. She'd spent many weeks with the man, and no one in the entirety of Avorstead had been immune to his charm and good looks. Including herself.

Then all her hopes and dreams crashed down on her when Yellow Skirt sighed. "The whole situation with his fiancée was unfortunate, wasn't it?"

Ivette's blood cooled, a pit sinking to the depths of her stomach. "He is engaged?"

"Was," Red Fan corrected. "She chose another man over him." She snapped her fan open. "Only the Mother Goddess knows why."

And then the man cocked his head to the side as he studied her. "What did you say your name was?"

"Ivette," she answered in a small tone, now overly aware of the stares she received from a few more passengers inside the wagon. How many had seen the precious cargo she carried?

"Well, Ivette… I'll save you the trouble of asking. The lord's ball is tomorrow evening, and rumor is he's looking for a wife."

The pit in her stomach only seemed to grow larger, tighter, more uncomfortable.

Blue Bonnet huffed. "It's not a rumor. It's the *law*. Everyone knows he's holding the ball to find a wife. It's no secret."

The wagon rumbled into a medium-sized town, and the driver reigned back the horses in front of a building with people waiting outside to board.

With a heavy heart and weary feet, Ivette gathered her belongings and stepped off the wagon. The moment her boots hit the ground, she glanced around at her surroundings. Things were a lot more…*blue* in Edilann than in Leonia. Blue drapes. Blue paint. Blue cloaks the soldiers wore secured to their breastplates.

She scanned the foreignness of her surroundings. Peddlers selling their wares. Groups of women gossiping in front of storefronts. Horses and wagons and carriages traversing the dirt roads.

When the pit in her stomach grew too heavy, she leaned against the railing of a storefront's porch to help support the weight of the escalating hurt within her heart.

Barnaby was searching for a *wife*. He was inviting every social class to his ball to find one. All while she was a perfectly willing candidate.

Was it against the law to marry someone from another kingdom? Or did he simply not want her in his life anymore?

Her gaze traveled from the way forward to the path that led back toward Leonia. A half hour's travel forward would take her into the heart of Edilann. Several days back would take her home.

She rubbed at the ache forming in her temples as all the shouts and laughter and clomping hooves attacked her ears and worsened the dull throbbing.

She'd come all this way. What could she possibly lose?

My heart.

Barnaby held the power to smash her heart into hundreds of pieces. She feared giving him the chance to wield the hammer. But if she returned home without seeing him, she knew she would regret it for the rest of her life.

So, she dug deep within herself to find the courage to take the first step forward. And then another. Until she followed the road at a brisk pace to make it to Edilann before sundown.

A yelp escaped her as an arm shot out from an alleyway and grabbed onto her wrist. She tried to scream as a man shoved her against a shadowed wall, but his grimy hand covered her mouth, muffling the sound.

"Hand over your bag," he growled menacingly.

She tried to knee him in the groin, but he blocked her attempt and pinned her harder to the wall until she whimpered with pain. She dropped the bag. But a second hand reached out to snatch it before the thief managed the feat. Her heart shot to her throat with the relief to find two Edilann guards.

"Release her," one of the guards ordered.

Her captor dropped his hand from her mouth, and he scrambled down the alleyway. However, the second guard sprinted after him and tackled him into the dirt before wrenching his arms behind his back and securing his wrists together.

Ivette barely managed to draw a breath before the first guard took her elbow and led her out of the alleyway. "You're coming with me."

"B-b-but I didn't do anything wrong!" she managed to gasp.

Unless…unless he knew about the pocket watch and ring she carried, possibly enough evidence to incriminate her as a thief despite her innocence.

She eyed her bag, which he still carried in a leather-clad hand. The watch and ring were in the pockets of her dress, but all of Barnaby's letters were tucked inside the bag. She could not bear to lose them.

The soldier led her across a smaller road where a black carriage rested beneath the shade of a large oak tree. A gold-painted crest of a rearing wildcat was emblazoned on the side, with two black and white horses waiting patiently as their driver fed them oats.

Fear struck her heart as the soldier handed back her bag, opened the coach door, and urged her inside.

The door slammed closed behind her, bathing her in disorienting darkness. At least until her eyes adjusted enough to notice the small table sitting in the middle of the carriage, and the woman staring unabashedly at her from where she sat on the bench opposite her, holding a teacup and saucer in her hands.

"I-I-I've done nothing wrong," Ivette stuttered, her hands trembling as she met the stare of the impeccably dressed woman before her. No one else sat in the carriage other than the two of them. "I am no thief."

The woman tipped her head to the side and cast her a disarming smile. "My name is Eloise. What is yours?"

"Ivette Danvers." She sat on her hands to hide the way they trembled.

After a few more moments, Eloise spoke again. "Do not take this the wrong way, dear." She placed her cup on her saucer and set it on the table between them. "You are not at all what I expected."

Despite her uncertainty of the situation, Ivette's face heated. "I don't know what you mean."

The woman gestured to the whole of her. "Your beauty is far from ordinary. But your hair..." She reached out and touched a strand, and Ivette tried not to flinch away. "What a beautiful shade of red." And then she cast her a warm smile. "I can see why my son is so heartbroken over losing you."

The breath halted in her lungs. She placed a hand over her racing heart as she stared back at the woman. Yes, there it was. The resemblance to Ben—Barnaby. The same shade of blond hair. Similar blue eyes and soft features.

"You're Ben's mother," she gasped, her previous fear and uncertainty fleeing altogether. But then she corrected herself when the woman raised an eyebrow. "I mean Barnaby."

"I am." Eloise chuckled and absently stirred her tea with a small spoon. Then, she reached for the teapot on the table, poured a second cup of tea, and placed it on a saucer in front of Ivette. "You are a smart young woman if you managed to figure out the truth on your own. He insisted he didn't want you to learn his true identity. It seems he didn't take your wits into account."

Shock coursed through her and chilled her blood. Placing her hands around the teacup allowed its warmth to seep into her cold fingers. "How did you…" Her words trailed off when she didn't know what, exactly, she wanted to ask.

"Oh…" The woman shrugged nonchalantly. "When he mentioned he met a woman, I simply had to know your name." Her mouth twitched before she took another sip of her tea. "I snooped into his belongings, and lo and behold, I found a stack of letters addressed to a woman he was clearly besotted with named Ivette." Another sip. "I've been secretly searching for you for weeks. My soldiers were to report to me if they heard any mention of the name 'Ivette.'"

"I never told anyone my name."

"Except on the wagon you were riding in." She laughed and shook her head, the blue in her eyes sparking with mischief. "I never imagined you were from Leonia. I should have set my sights a bit broader than Edilann."

Ivette lowered her gaze, still trying to make sense of the situation. "Why?"

"Is that not obvious, dear?" She laughed before reaching across the table with a gloved hand and placing it on top of hers. "I want you to marry my son. And I almost always get what I want."

Chapter Fourteen

"This is where you live?" Ivette gasped as the carriage rolled up to an enormous estate three stories tall with more windows than she could count. Two towers rose up on either side of the house—which she could only possibly describe as a castle—with reddish-gray stone walls and several spires shooting from the tops of the roof.

Her breath caught at the expansive gardens on either side of the estate filled with a variety of colorful, blooming flowers, trees, and shrubs, managed by a handful of servants. She eyed the neat jumble of roses in different shades. In Avorstead, she'd only seen roses a couple of times.

The carriage pulled around to the side of the estate, allowing her to see more of the grounds. A beautiful white arch teaming with climbing flowers led into another part of the garden, and she only wished to explore the depths of the winding paths.

But first…

Barnaby.

"Now, don't be alarmed by the number of servants inside," Eloise said as a footman opened the carriage door. "We are preparing for a ball tomorrow, so there are a lot more than usual out and about."

The man stuck out a hand and helped Eloise down and next, Ivette. She glanced around in wonder as they entered beneath a stone arch, climbed several stairs, and stepped through a door another servant held open for them, which led into what appeared to be a massive kitchen. Several ovens. Tables. Masses of food. And even more servants preparing the food.

Each dipped their heads in acknowledgement. Ivette tried to protest such treatment, but Eloise guided her quickly through the kitchens and into a large hallway.

"This reminds me of my courting days with my late husband, John," the other woman giggled, gloved hand pressed to her mouth. "Don't want to get caught."

"By whom?"

"Barnaby, of course. It will ruin everything I have planned if he discovers us. And he's scheduled to arrive home in just a few minutes."

"But—"

However, before she managed to speak, Eloise guided her up a set of stairs climbing one of two walls to the next floor. They entered another hallway, this one decorated with lavish paintings, small tables with vases or plants, and beautiful drapes without a speck of dirt marring the white fabric. The corridor slanted left to form a square shape with doors sparsely placed on her right.

Eloise twisted the handle of one of the doors and pushed it open. Ivette inhaled sharply.

An ornate mantle framed a fireplace directly to her left, and to her right lay a bed large enough for herself and all her sisters to occupy, draped with a velvet canopy over the four-post bed frame.

"Now, you must forgive me for not placing you closer to the family suites," Eloise said as she steered her through a smaller door to the side of the bed and into…well, she wasn't sure what it was. She'd never seen one before. "The guest suites will do well enough for now, and if you ever have any need of a servant, just ring this bell and one will come calling."

Ivette turned in a full circle, overcome by awe. A claw-foot bathtub rested in the middle of the small room with a drying cloth draped over a chair and a nightgown and slippers lying on top of it.

A variety of soaps and perfumes rested within a wicker cupboard, and when she dipped her fingers into the water of the tub, she pulled it back quickly and gasped.

"It's warm!"

Eloise laughed, her blue eyes sparkling with amusement in a similar way Barnaby's did. It made her miss him even more. "Yes, well, I do hope you have the chance to get used to it." She stepped closer, and her levity transitioned into seriousness. "I only have one rule for you."

"Anything."

The woman gave her a stern look. "Barnaby cannot know you are here until tomorrow night at the ball."

"Why not? If I could just speak to him—"

"My dear, this has nothing to do with you or him. But rather everything to do with society."

"I don't...understand?" She suddenly felt like a fool traversing a foreign world with rules she could not seem to comprehend. This entire situation could be smoothed over with a conversation. She didn't want to play games.

The woman fixed a flyaway hair on Ivette's head. "Considering your background... The way you are presented means everything for a first impression. Everyone must believe you and Barnaby are a love match. No one can refute your station in such a case should you become the next countess of Willowbloom Hall. It all comes down to his reaction to you."

"A-a-and..." Her voice quavered. "What if he does not have a favorable reaction?"

Eloise gripped her hand and squeezed. "Do you love my son?"

"More than anything," she breathed, but then her face flushed with heat at her confession. But thankfully, the woman only smiled.

"Then you must be brave. Courage will get you far enough. And if you mean as much to him as he does to you, he will meet you halfway."

"How can you be so certain?" She averted her gaze in an attempt to hide her hurt. "He left me."

"And that boy's been sulking ever since. He made a mistake, and he knows it. Just give him a chance to correct it."

The woman literally floated from the room and paused at the open door of the bedroom. "Servants will come and go with your meals. Clothing is in the armoire. Books and stationery on the desk. I will return tomorrow afternoon with something for you to wear for the ball."

"You really don't have to—"

But Eloise closed the door before she finished her sentence, leaving her too stunned to do anything more than release a tense breath. Of course, she couldn't go to a fancy ball wearing the clothes she'd brought with her to Edilann. It hadn't been her intent to attend a ball at all. But if Eloise thought this was the best course of action, then she trusted her.

Ivette stripped herself of her stiff, dirtied clothing and dipped herself into the bathtub. She sighed as the luxurious heat washed over her, and she sank lower to soak herself before she washed her hair with a white soap that gave her strands a silky texture. Next, she scrubbed the dirt from her legs, hands, and beneath her fingernails. Six days had been a long time on the road without a proper bath.

She regretfully stepped out of the tub, dried off, and changed into the nightgown and slippers. When she returned to the room, she was surprised to find her clothing gone, and in their place was a tray of steaming soup and a chunk of bread sitting on the bedside table.

"Is this how you truly live?" she couldn't help but surmise, stirring the soup and inhaling its fresh, earthy fragrance. People to bring him food, to wash his clothes, to fill his bath. It was…heavenly. The idea of focusing on herself and what *she* wanted to do with her time rather than scraping by just to survive was immensely appealing.

By the time she finished the meal, darkness had descended upon the kingdom. Surely, everyone else must be asleep or at least retired to their rooms.

She turned the door handle, and the door opened silently. Taking a deep breath, she dared to peek her head outside, only to find a flicker of candlelight in the sconces to illuminate the corridor in a dim glow.

She stole across the lush carpet and tiptoed downstairs, pausing every so often to listen to her surroundings. Faint whispers reached her ears, likely from the servants within the estate. Laughter from farther away echoed down the common area below the stairs. The clinking of dishes and silverware sounded from the kitchens.

"Eloise only gave me one rule," she reminded herself under her breath when she thought she might be doing something wrong by walking the hallways at night. Therefore, she wrapped her shawl tighter around herself, stole through the kitchen area while simultaneously trying not to bring attention to herself, and exited the estate through the back entrance.

A rush of crisp, fresh air greeted her, and she inhaled a deep breath, taking in the different scents of a new location. Sweet flowers. Freshly cut grass. The scent of rich bark and overturned earth.

A smile on her face, she followed the path into the garden under the cover of darkness, taking in the beautiful blooms glowing beneath the moonlight overhead.

She pulled her slippers off, afraid to dirty them as she continued down the path. More than once, she stopped to smell a rose or to touch the silky petals of a chamomile plant. She wandered deeper and deeper into the garden, only wishing the sun was out to give her a better view of the pops of color and alluring atmosphere.

But then she froze at the sound of flipping paper.

A part of her knew she should turn back, to avoid being seen by anyone. At least until tomorrow. But the other part of her couldn't help but venture forward on silent feet until she peered around a garden trellis to find a stone bench lit up by the light from a lantern, as well as illuminating the man sitting on top.

Ivette's blood froze with shock. She recognized the blond sweep of the man's hair. The broad shoulders. The way his shirt dipped low to expose the top of his chest. And she would never forget his face.

But unlike in Avorstead, it was not a happy face. A deep melancholy rested in Barnaby's expression as he turned another paper over. With a start, she realized he was reading her letters.

You do *still care…*

Even more, he was here. He truly was Barnaby Allistair Mavis like she'd pieced together. Seeing him in the flesh at Willowbloom Hall only solidified her findings.

She wanted to storm through the flower arch and give him a piece of her mind, and then kiss him senseless and beg him to reconsider. But…

"I only have one rule for you."

Reluctantly, she backed away from the arch, glancing at him one last time before returning the way she came. She feared he might propose to another woman before she had a chance to see him again.

But if what Eloise said was true… Then she must wait.

Chapter Fifteen

Throughout the day, Ivette worried and fretted and wrung her hands until they bled. She could nearly make out the trail from her pacing embedded within the carpet. She almost wished she had arrived today rather than yesterday to ensure she didn't have enough time to concoct every possible scenario in her head. Barnaby's acceptance of her. His refusal. His dismissal. Perhaps disdain.

If he rejected her in public, she would be mortified.

"Have courage and be strong," she whispered to herself throughout her confinement in her room. Eloise never said she couldn't leave. Only that Barnaby couldn't know she was there. But she knew leaving posed a risk to Eloise's trust in her. Although she didn't do well with sitting still and staying in one place, it was only for one day.

She took a seat beside the window as afternoon transitioned to dusk. Her heart shot to her throat when she spotted carriages rolling down the drive and approaching the estate, only for beautifully dressed men and women to step out.

Her breath caught at the stunning reds and blues and greens of ball gowns, and the impeccably dressed men in black and white and some in other colors like blue or red. She possessed nothing of the sort to make her look like a princess herself.

Someone knocked on the door, making her jump. Moments later, a plump woman entered, her face flushed red with fluster. "Please forgive my tardiness," she said with a hasty curtsy before she closed the door behind her and strode into the room carrying a bag in her hands. "The king and queen arrived only an hour ago."

Ivette's face paled. "King and queen?" she squeaked.

The woman nodded as she pushed her into a chair and began to work a miracle on her hair with deft hands and a variety of pins. "They were not expected, you see." A pin in her mouth slurred her words. "We've been scrambling to ensure their comfort at Willowbloom Hall. The missus said you were the number one priority but can't exactly make the royal family number two."

"Are they here for the ball?"

Laughing, the woman said, "Everyone who matters is here at the ball." But then she flushed all over again. "Forgive me, miss. I meant no offense."

It was clear the woman hinted at her rank in society. Or lack of. But Ivette already knew she was out of place. She surely felt out of place amongst beautiful people in beautiful gowns.

"Just one more…there!" The woman beamed, proud of her own work, before she turned Ivette to face the mirror.

She inhaled sharply at the image staring back at her. Half of her hair was pinned up in an intricate twist, while the rest fell flatteringly over her shoulder in beautiful waves. Of course, the waves were a product of her bath from last night, but somehow, the woman had managed to tame the strands and make them shimmer in an elegant manner.

"Thank you!" she exclaimed. "You are so very talented."

Once again, the woman flushed red but didn't get an opportunity to accept her thanks before the door opened again and Eloise entered carrying a large bundle in her arms. The woman bowed out of the room, and Barnaby's mother took her place.

"It's been a hectic day and the night hasn't even started!" Eloise laughed as she draped the bundle over the bed, taking up a good portion of the space. "I wore this dress at my engagement ball, and I thought it would complement your coloring beautifully."

Eloise untied the knot at the bottom of the cloth bag and revealed a shimmer of silver within. The sight stole her breath away as she uncovered the rest to reveal a sleeveless silver gown with a satin ribbon across the top of the bodice that would drape over her shoulders when worn. Beads and silver silk flowers adorned the bodice, dripping down into the full skirt like wisterias climbing over a delicate garden arch.

"I can't possibly wear this," she managed to say in a breathless tone, running her hand reverently down the silky fabric. "This is an important dress."

"Which is precisely why you *should* wear it."

Despite her protesting, Eloise helped her into the gown, buttoned it at the back, and turned her to face the mirror.

Shock slammed into her when she gazed back at a completely foreign person. The woman staring back at her was beautiful with elegant hair, charming freckles, and a stunning ball gown. Gone was her simple outfit and unruly mane.

A pit of anxiety formed in her stomach when she thought about what she must do tonight. The dress certainly made everything feel…real. Consequential. Terrifying.

"I'm scared," Ivette admitted. "If Barnaby wanted me, he would have come back."

Eloise stood behind her and draped a strand of pearls around her neck.

"My son has a misconstrued idea that he is worthless." A pause. "Let me tell you what he was like as a child. And plenty of it is his father's fault, mind you. He would get praise for something done perfectly and ignored if he made a mistake. Therefore, he was really hard on himself if he couldn't be perfect. He has made mistakes, and he is finding it difficult to forgive himself."

"Does this have to do with his former betrothed?"

Eloise's fingers stilled on a pearl comb sitting on the table beside them, her expression troubled. "Partly," she answered finally. "I never met Mirabelle. She was a commoner, like you, and ended up marrying a palace guard."

"What happened?" she whispered.

The other woman tucked the comb into her hair and reached for a pair of silver, elbow-length gloves next. "His father passed away a few months before he met Mirabelle, and Barnaby was not in a good place. He became…unrecognizable. His father was gone, the person he had admired most in the world. And as the heir, so much responsibility had been thrust upon him so suddenly, almost without warning." She helped Ivette into one glove and then the other. "It didn't help that the king was putting pressure on him to marry. Barnaby…well, he broke. He found unhealthy ways to cope with his stress, and he met Mirabelle at the wrong time in his life, during the thick of his hurting."

Eloise smoothed a strand of Ivette's hair near her ear and continued. "I don't know exactly what happened, but I suspect he may have said or done something to drive her away. He's been trying his utmost hardest to stop drinking and take over the business affairs where his father left off." She smiled. "He's the Barnaby I remember again. Except…he's sad. And I don't like to see my child sad."

Ivette frowned at the thought of his hurt. She wanted to take away his pain. "I've seen his good, kind heart. I know how good of a man he is because he's shown me time and again." She smoothed a hand over the beautiful silver dress, feeling like a fraud wearing it. She was a sheep girl who mended clothing and churned butter and milked cows. She was not…*this*.

"They will see right through me," she said in a hoarse voice, her fingers trailing over her freckles and to her bare shoulders, making her feel far too exposed despite the beauty of the gown. "I am not what a countess should be."

But Eloise lifted her chin and urged her to look at herself in the mirror. "You are a *sight*. And it doesn't matter what you *think* you should be. Because what you *are* is enough." She straightened the pearl necklace over Ivette's collarbones. "The dress will tell everyone you are *my* choice. It's all the credibility you need."

Ivette's chin trembled, her eyes shimmering with tears. She spun around and threw her arms around Eloise, holding her tight as she tried her best not to let her tears fall. For so many years, she had acted as her sisters' mother. She hadn't realized how desperately she needed a mother herself.

The sweet woman produced a handkerchief and dabbed at Ivette's cheeks despite her attempts to keep her tears from spilling. And then she kissed her forehead as a mother might do for her daughter.

"Dry yourself up and head on down to the ball when you're ready." She moved gracefully toward the door and stopped in the doorway to cast her a smile. "But try not to wait too long. I don't think Barnaby can handle the strain of your absence for much longer."

And then the door shut behind her. The resounding silence made her overly aware of her own pulse pounding through her ears and the heat of anxiety climbing her neck. Fleeing with her sisters had been difficult. Taking care of them and becoming their support was one of her hardest sacrifices. But somehow, standing in front of a room filled with beautiful, wealthy people after showing up at Barnaby's house unannounced seemed like the hardest thing she'd had yet to face.

"I can't do this…" She pulled off one of her gloves and wrung it between her hands as she paced the room. "I can't do this…"

But if she didn't, some other woman would take her place tonight, and she'd forever regret not taking one more courageous step.

I can't do this.

Barnaby's stomach twisted with knots of nausea and unease, becoming worse the longer he remained on the ballroom floor. *Hundreds* of young ladies with scheming mothers had shown up at the ball, and just as he escaped one group of women huddling around him, he accidentally walked into another.

He winced as one persistent matron dug her long fingernails into his arm as she steered him toward her three daughters dressed in gaudy colors with feathers flying wildly from their hair. He wanted to wrench himself out of her grip. He wanted to dig his heels into the floor.

He wanted to run away.

But the king and queen kept watching him from where they stood in their own corner of the ballroom graciously greeting guests within their circle. He couldn't make a scene. Not when they were here.

Across the room, his friends pointed at him and laughed, their voices nearly drowned by the music, dancing feet, and cacophony of conversation. What he wanted to do was give them the bird. But he settled for a nasty glare instead.

It only encouraged their laughter to grow louder.

Barnaby spat out a feather that flitted past his mouth, and his disgruntlement grew when three young ladies entered his personal space. Touching him and breathing the same air. He took a polite step back, but they only followed with one step forward as they peacocked and chattered and boasted of their talents and accomplishments.

Please save me, he silently begged his friends. Of course, they only hooted with laughter, clearly enjoying the show.

The collage of colorful skirts, flitting feathers, and deafening voices caused his head to spin. Heat spiked through his chest and to his neck. His face flushed with discomfort at the overwhelming number of people surrounding him. The music became too loud. The lights too bright.

He was about to spin on his heel when someone slipped an arm through his. He almost wrenched it away until he glanced down to find his mother's familiar, welcome face at his shoulder.

"Excuse me, ladies," his mother said with an apologetic smile. "I must steal my son away for a few minutes. Please, do enjoy the party."

"Where have you been?" he hissed under his breath as she led him away. "I'm being bombarded with young ladies from all over the kingdom that *you* invited. I think you should be the one to scare them away."

His mother giggled behind a gloved hand. "A few young ladies have your feathers ruffled?"

He scowled. "It's not them. It's their tenacious mothers who throw their daughters at me." When she made a face, he insisted, "No, really. One of them actually shoved their daughter into my arms. If I wasn't the gentleman that I am, I would have let her fall instead."

She patted his arm sympathetically. "It must be a burden to be such a sought-after bachelor." But then she tipped her head toward the opposite side of the room, closer to where the king and queen resided. "I managed to divide the room into strangers and people in our circle. I think you will be more comfortable over here."

But as she led him beneath the sparkling chandelier and toward a group of ladies he recognized from other social events, his palms broke out in a cold sweat. His ears became stuffy as if plugged with cotton, muffling the music and voices around him. His heart raced. His world spun. And when each breath quickened with dread, his mother tightened her grip on his elbow.

"Barnaby, are you all right?"

"No," he gasped. "I can't stay here. I can't do this."

He could not marry another. He needed Ivette like he needed air to breathe, legs to walk, light to see.

Understanding reached her eyes, and rather than insisting for him to remain, she steered him in another direction. "We'll make a calm exit to our right. Keep it together for thirty more seconds."

The exit seemed much too far away. He never thought he was the type, but he thought he might faint.

"Deep breaths," she encouraged.

They were almost there, but he feared he might not make it when he suddenly felt too lightheaded to keep his feet beneath his body. Just when he thought he might succumb to fainting, two words echoed from the top of the staircase where the announcer trumpeted the next arrival.

"Ivette Danvers!"

Hyperawareness flooded him as if he'd heard his own name. Barnaby's eyes widened, and his head snapped toward the staircase. All at once, his surroundings ceased spinning. His heart calmed. His breaths evened out.

He blinked several times to try to make sense of the beautiful apparition standing at the top of the stairs. A sparkling silver dress shimmered beneath the crystalline candlelight. Long, copper hair draped over one of her slender shoulders. And his heart nearly capsized when his gaze rested on her heart-shaped face.

His jaw slackened. His breath faltered.

Ivette was no apparition. She was real.

And like a moth drawn to a flame, he could not help but release his mother's arm and step toward the staircase.

Chapter Sixteen

Pure terror climbed into Ivette's chest and whipped her heart into an overly fast rhythm not at all in sync with the musicians set up on a short stage in the corner of the ballroom. *Hundreds* of people stood below, not just a few dozen like she'd expected.

And when the man at the top of the stairs announced her name, numerous eyes glanced in her direction and remained there. Watching her. Staring.

Her eyes widened as she froze to the spot.

She didn't know what to do. Where to go. How to traverse this new, strange world.

Fear won the battle over bravery. And just as she turned to flee, something caught fast onto her hand.

She inhaled a sharp intake of breath as she spun around, only for her heart to leap to her throat when she gazed into a pair of familiar blue eyes. Her gaze fluttered over Barnaby's face, his hair, and his eyes once again, and it was as if a wave of relief crashed over her. She'd spent an entire week searching for him, and even longer fretting over his well-being and her broken heart.

But he was whole and safe and impossibly more handsome than she remembered him.

"I told you not to look for me," he breathed, and she didn't miss the way his gaze lingered on her lips before meeting her eye once again.

She replied breathlessly. "How could I let you go so easily?" Somehow, she fought against the tremors that threatened to shiver through her body as she reached into the pocket of her dress and pulled out his pocket watch. She dared to take a chance by slipping it into the breast pocket of his dress coat.

A perfect fit.

When she lifted her gaze, she was overly aware of the lack of music and the astonished murmurs echoing from below. "Besides, you still owe me a dance."

"I do, don't I?" His hand gripped hers tighter, but he made no further movement. He lowered his voice to a husky whisper. "You are the most stunning creature to ever walk these halls."

Heat blossomed in her cheeks as she glanced over his shoulder to the throngs of beautiful women below. "You can't mean that." Another knot formed in her stomach, refusing to abate. "Besides, you say that to all the girls."

"I have not danced with a single one of them tonight." His fingers skimmed over her temple and tucked a strand of hair behind her ear. "There is only you."

"You didn't even know I would be here."

"I admit I am…shocked." He moved close enough for her to feel his minty breath on her cheek. "I cannot possibly survive another moment without you. Promise not to leave my side."

She swallowed, not knowing if it was a promise she could keep. Because in the end, he had still left her. And she didn't know where she stood with him.

So, she simply smiled and returned the squeeze of his hand.

He seemed to take it as an agreement, as he turned and guided her down the stairs, making her appear elegant when her wobbly legs threatened to collapse with each step down the staircase.

Guests clapped as he led her into the middle of the dance floor and signaled to the musicians with his fingers, the number four and then the number one. To her horror, no one joined them. But rather, they created a large circle around them to watch.

"I can't dance!" she gasped quietly.

He responded by pulling her close with one hand clasped around hers and his other around her waist. He leaned near enough to whisper in her ear. "This will be just like in Avorstead. All you need to do is trust me and follow my lead."

"How will I know you won't leave me by myself on the dance floor?"

Barnaby released a long breath and briefly closed his eyes just as the music started, seeming to realize she wasn't simply talking about the dance at all.

He stepped forward, and she followed his lead and stepped back as he led her in a dance. She became quiet for several beats as she tried to focus on her footwork and not misstepping in a different direction he didn't lead her.

"How did you find me?" he asked quietly instead of answering her question.

He spun her out, and a chorus of "oooh"s and "awww"s lifted into the air around them when her skirts fanned out in a mesmerizing shimmer. When she spun back into his side, she said, "It took me an entire week to figure it out after we received your generous pardon from our debts. I searched for Ben for days. Until I received a tip that the ring I found on my property belonged to an earl. After that, I managed to connect the dots, and it brought me here." Her mouth twitched. "Well, your *mother* brought me here. It seems she was looking for me as well."

For several beats, his mouth went slack as if too stunned to speak. "I thought this was my mother's dress. That conniving woman." He chuckled, his smile lighting up his face in a way that inspired a few more "oooh"s and "awww"s from the crowd. She almost laughed. Almost. Because the sight caused her knees to go weak as well.

In her momentary distraction, she accidentally stepped on the hem of the dress and gasped as she clung onto him. But rather than falling, he dipped her elegantly at the waist as if the move had been preconceived.

But rather than straightening, he held her in the dip, and she found herself ensnared by the blue of his eyes, by the gentle touch of his hands, by the soft curve of his mouth.

"I do not have enough control for this," he said in a strained tone. "If I continue holding you for a second more, I'm going to kiss you."

A shuddering breath of anticipation escaped her. "A kiss doesn't sound too awful."

Barnaby closed his eyes for a mere moment before he straightened them both. He signaled to the musicians again, and they struck up a different tune. A faster tune. And only then did others start to form a circle for a dance while curiosity still lingered on their faces.

Next, he glanced across the room, and she followed his gaze to find him speaking in silent gestures to his mother, who watched them with a sheen of joy in her eyes. She simply nodded and dabbed at her eyes with a handkerchief before she moved in the opposite direction.

He gripped her hand and pulled her across the room, past moon-eyed girls and disappointed matrons.

"What did you tell your mother?" she asked, keeping up with his long, hurried strides.

He glanced sideways at her and grinned. "To keep guards stationed at the doors. I want you all to myself for a few minutes."

Unable to help herself, she returned his grin as he pulled her through a set of double-glass doors and outside onto the empty balcony. A guard closed the door behind them, a faint light from inside filtering through the glass and bathing them in a dim glow.

A few breaths passed between them, and then they reached for each other at the same time as if the time apart had made them desperate for the other.

Barnaby crushed his lips against hers, and she responded by clutching onto the front of his coat to pull him as close to her as possible. She met each fevered kiss with desperation, holding on tightly, afraid he might disappear if she let go.

He backed her away from the windows and into the shadows until her shoulders brushed against the cool stone of the wall. He took a hold of her hands and pinned them above her head, slowly sliding his fingers over her palms, her wrists, down her arms, her sides, until he gripped her hips and pulled her closer.

"I love you, Ivette," he murmured against her lips. "I love you with every fiber of my heart." He kissed her jaw. "Of my soul." He kissed her throat. "I have not stopped thinking about you for a moment in our weeks apart."

His words left her dazed, and his lips grazing her skin made it difficult to form a coherent thought. But as much as she wanted to kiss him until both of her feet floated on golden clouds, she knew they had too much to talk about.

She threaded her fingers through his hair and kissed him again on the lips. Slowly this time. Savoring his touch. His kiss. Cooling their feverish need into a flickering warmth.

"You broke my heart," she murmured. He stilled against her, but she didn't allow it to deter them as she placed a gentle kiss on his jaw and smoothed a hand down his chest.

"I would rather kiss than talk," he said, but she didn't miss the layer of guilt in his voice.

"You know we can't."

He sighed. "I know."

He held either side of her face and gazed down at her, his thumbs brushing her cheekbones like the light touch of a feather. He opened his mouth, but no words escaped as if he wasn't sure what to say.

"When did you get your memories back?" she asked, holding his wrists to discourage him from pulling away from her again. "How?"

His throat bobbed with a swallow before his gaze averted to the stone wall behind her. "My friends found me in town." Another swallow. "They said some things that triggered my memories. One of the friends is Charles. He's the…uh…sheep thief."

Ivette dropped her hands when the shock of the information rained over her head. She recalled the rustlers. Little Helen getting trapped in the stampede. Barnaby, then Ben, risking himself to save her.

"All right," she said slowly, taking in the new information. "So, you have questionable friends."

A shiver ran over her arms when he dropped his hands from her face and stepped away. A long breath escaped him as he leaned against the stone ledge of the balcony and stared out over the silhouettes of the horizon.

She joined him, forcing herself to place distance between them lest they resume their fiery kiss.

"I never said I condone the things he does. They're wrong. What happened with Helen was extremely unfortunate. Believe me when I say I boxed his ears and threw dung in his face." He chuckled and shook his head. "Actually, all three of us threw dung in his face. He certainly deserved it. He smelled like arse for an entire week."

But then he sobered, and his smile dropped into a frown. "I meant what I said. In my goodbye letter."

"I disagree." She placed a hand on his arm, and his gaze darted to her as if surprised by the contact. Chirping crickets filled the momentary silence between them before she continued. "Being a good man and having a good heart are different from the mistakes you've made in the past." She squeezed his bicep. "Making mistakes doesn't make you a bad man; it makes you human."

He hung his head. "You don't know the things I've done. I…was engaged before you."

"I know." It must have been bad if he felt so much shame over the past. "But I don't care what you've done before you met me." How could she possibly explain how she felt? What he meant to her? "All I care about is the way you treated my sisters with such love and respect. The way you helped us look after the property and livestock. The way you brought joy and laughter into our lives." She brushed her fingers beneath his chin and lifted his head. "You did that, Barnaby."

He placed his hand on top of hers and sighed. "I like that."

"Like what?"

Another smile graced his mouth as he took her hand and kissed each of her fingers. "I like it when you call me by my name. I knew Ben didn't sound quite right."

His gaze met hers, and once again, a heavy silence lingered between them. She was here. She'd said what she needed to say. But what more could she do? Was this the end for them?

Eloise's words came to mind.

"If you mean as much to him as he does to you, he will meet you halfway."

But what if he didn't? He'd confessed his love for her. Was it enough?

She reached into her pocket until her fingers clasped around the ring that had fallen from her sheep's mouth. Very softly, she placed it onto the balcony between them with a soft *plink.*

Barnaby stared at the ring for the longest time, and she only wished to know what thoughts whirled in his mind.

"One of my sheep found it," she explained. "I assumed it belonged to you." When he continued to stare at the ring, she ducked her head and wrapped her arms around herself. He wasn't going to meet her halfway. He was going to break her heart again.

Emotion pricked at her eyes, but she managed to hold herself together. It was a risk coming here. She knew it from the beginning. What chance did she have with an *earl*? She was just a simple sheep girl with no money, no title, and certainly no status in society.

"I came to thank you," she said when he still didn't speak. "You saved us from financial ruin. I am so grateful to you. My sisters are as well."

More silence.

"Will you at least say something?"

Barnaby cleared his throat and cleared it again. "I have a hard time speaking when I can't say it perfectly right. I don't know how to word this. I don't want to mess it up."

She recalled what Eloise had told her about him, about him being hard on himself when he couldn't do something perfectly. "Then fumble through it." Somehow, she managed a smile. "Give yourself some grace."

After several long moments, he reached into a pocket inside his dress coat, and her heart caught when he placed an exquisite gold ring with a matching red ruby center like his own onto the ledge. Her lips parted as she glanced from the ring to his face. She didn't find guilt or shame or uncertainty like she expected. But rather determination. Confidence. Relief.

"I have been trying so hard to become a man worthy of my title. Worthy of you. I wish I could have more time to prove to you that I can take care of your heart. But I have no more time to spare." He reached over the rings and placed his hand on top of hers.

Her breath fled at his touch, her heart pounding through every facet of her body.

"What…what are you saying?" she asked breathlessly.

His mouth pulled into a smile as he laughed. "I'm fumbling through a marriage proposal. You knocked me flat on my face tonight by showing up. Some warning may have been nice."

"Your mother insisted I give you no warning," she said, returning his laugh. But then she edged forward cautiously. "If I hadn't shown up tonight, would this ring have ended up on another woman's finger?"

Laughter burst out of him, and he shook his head in a self-deprecating way. "I was on the verge of panic mere moments before you showed up at the top of the stairs. I would have ridden out this very night, all the way to Avorstead, and begged for your forgiveness. Because I realized I could not live without you." His smile lingered as he trailed his fingers over her cheek. "And it seems my mother realized it far earlier than I did."

"Barnaby…" she whispered.

He kissed one side of her mouth. "Marry me, Ivette." And then he kissed the other side. "We'll face all the adventures of life together."

A breath shuddered out of her at his most pleasant touch. "There is no question about my answer. Yes. Absolutely, yes."

Barnaby wasted no time before he slowly pulled her glove off her hand and slipped the engagement ring onto her finger.

Although his ring was one of duty rather than love, she slid it onto his pinky finger as well.

And then he took her by surprise as he grabbed her around the waist and spun her around. She giggled at the elation of being in his arms, at being his forever. He quickly stifled her laughter with a kiss, and then another, until her feet floated on a golden cloud of happiness.

"Smashing my head open was the best thing to have ever happened to me," he murmured into her hair as he pulled her close.

She sighed and rested her head against his chest, feeling his heartbeat against her ear, enjoying the warmth he offered. "Don't ever let it happen again."

He laughed and gave her one last kiss. "Let's go back inside together and allow me to introduce the future Lady Mavis to my peers."

"That sounds terrifying, but…I trust you." She took his hand and squeezed it. "I love you, Barnaby Allistair Mavis."

He kissed her wrist and then her finger wearing his ring. "And I love you. Always."

Chapter Seventeen

"*Please*, stop torturing me!" Barnaby grinned as he leaned against the doorframe of the closed door, the girls within giggling at his playful impatience. "I have been waiting *all* day."

The door opened and Senna's head stuck out. "You will just have to wait a few more minutes. She's almost ready."

And when she slammed the door in his face, the giggling ensued. He rolled his eyes when he recognized one of the giggles belonging to his mother. It was as if five new girls living in their home coaxed a youthful side out of her. She'd always wanted daughters. And now she had more than she'd bargained for.

The giggling transitioned into excited whispers, and his heart skipped with nervous anticipation. The door opened again, and this time little Helen exited the room.

"Turn around," she ordered. "And close your eyes."

He chuckled when he did as he was told. She guided him down the hallway and placed him ten paces away from the door. He clasped his hands behind his back while focusing on taking deep breaths. He was ready for this. He was ready for his bride.

"Remember…no peeking!"

Oh, it was certainly difficult not to take a little peek. Especially when he heard the swish of skirts on the other end of the corridor and a sharp intake of breath. He hadn't seen Ivette in an entire day. Of course, it seemed like so little time in comparison to a lifetime together. But it was pure torture.

"You can turn around now," Senna said.

Taking a steadying breath, Barnaby opened his eyes and slowly turned.

His breath caught when his gaze landed on his beautiful bride. Ivette wore a white, lacy dress with loose sleeves draping off either shoulder. Beads lined the lacy bodice, the cut of the gown flattering her figure. A blue-jeweled necklace lay at her throat. Her copper hair was pinned up, with several curls escaping the ensemble and brushing against her skin.

His gaze traveled over the path of light freckles on her shoulders, up her neck, and to her face. A lump lodged itself in his throat as he gazed into her beautiful hazel eyes, the sudden realization that he'd be gazing into them for the rest of his life.

A month's engagement had been far too long, and somehow, waiting even less than an hour now to marry her was just as torturous.

He crossed the space between them in several strides, but just as he reached out to touch her, his mother swatted him playfully with a fan. "No touching. If you ruin her hair, you will have me to contend with."

He shook his head in disbelief, never breaking eye contact with his intended. "You cruel, cruel women. Such teases."

But he ignored the rule anyway and gently cradled her face in his hands, whispering so only she could hear. "I'll see you at the altar." And then he kissed her lips lightly, sweetly. "You look absolutely radiant."

Ivette smiled and whispered just as quietly, "I won't make you wait too long. The Mother Goddess knows you've waited too long already. You've certainly bemoaned about it enough."

Laughing, he kissed her one last time before striding down the hallway, knowing if he stayed any longer, her hair would most certainly get mussed by his hands.

He hoped he wouldn't have to wait much longer to wed his bride. Otherwise, he wouldn't be able to help himself from bemoaning a little more.

A shaky exhale left Ivette's lips as she stood behind the corner of the chapel doors, focusing on taking deep breaths as a string quartet played music from within. The lovely melody met her ears, reminding her of *who* she was marrying.

An earl. Her handsome, amazing Barnaby.

White and pink roses spilled out of the doors with large, white ribbons keeping the flowers together in magnificent bouquets. Barnaby had gone through extra lengths to make sure she had exactly what she wanted for the wedding. While the only thing she had requested was him and her sisters present at the ceremony, he'd inquired of her favorite flower, her favorite colors, her favorite instruments, and even her favorite foods.

He clearly wanted to make the wedding perfect for her. But truly, all she needed was him.

But the flowers *did* make her quite happy as well.

Beside her, Eloise dabbed at her eyes, which she'd done all morning long, and wrapped her arms around her and held on tight. "Welcome to the family, dear."

She laughed and tried not to let her own tears fall. "I'm not quite there."

"When else would I be able to express my happiness?" The woman chuckled and squeezed Ivette's hand. "Barnaby will commandeer every moment with you for the rest of the day. I'm sure of it."

"I am truly happy to be here."

With one last embrace, Eloise entered the chapel to take a seat before the ceremony started. Only then did her eyes smart at how…*alone*…she felt. Her father was gone. She had no brothers. Vincent couldn't attend the wedding because his wife had given birth to their fourth son. And she wasn't close enough with anyone else from Avorstead for them to walk her down the aisle.

Rambunctious laughter from behind caused her to spin around, only to find Barnaby's three mischievous friends—Charles, Edward, and Tobie—approaching while shoving each other's shoulders as if they'd just shared a quip.

Ivette placed her hands on her hips and scowled. "You owe me two sheep, Charles."

"Shh, shh, shh." He held a finger to his lips and glanced over his shoulder. "I'll do you better than two sheep. How about a horse?"

She released an exasperated sigh. Even Barnaby didn't know much about Charles' exploits, but the man likely didn't have the sheep anymore. She didn't know *where* he would get said horse, so she didn't accept his offer.

"An apology would do just fine."

"I'm sorr—"

"To my youngest sister, Helen. I have no need of it."

Charles huffed. "Fine, fine, fine. Later today." And then he held out an arm to her. She eyed it suspiciously.

"What are you doing?"

To her other side, Edward answered while he, too, offered an arm. "Walking you down the aisle, you dunderhead—" Tobie smacked him across the head. "Ow! I mean, beautiful, magnificent woman, you."

Ivette laughed, her eyes smarting all over again. She hardly knew these men, but they were here for her when no one else could be, standing in for the men who couldn't or wouldn't.

She gratefully took either of their arms while Tobie held the train of her dress behind her.

The music picked up its rhythm, giving her the signal to proceed through the doors. She inhaled a long breath and released it slowly. Dozens of nobles waited around the corner, including the king and queen of Edilann. To say she was nervous was an understatement.

But…

She would do this. For Barnaby. Because she loved him and wanted to spend the rest of her life with him.

Taking one last steadying breath, she pulled her veil over her face and stepped forward with the two men on either side of her. They entered through the doors of the chapel, between two large bouquets of pink and white roses. Everyone seated on either side of the pews stood in her presence, the ground seeming to shake with the movement.

Her pulse raced. Her steps faltered.

But then she spotted Barnaby standing at the front of the room, his mouth hanging open as he got to see the rest of the ensemble of the dress Eloise had so generously made to her specifications, the garment finished only barely within the month of her engagement.

As she gazed at her handsome fiancé—soon to be husband—her heart calmed, and her legs steadied. He wore a tailored black suit with a light blue cravat tied around his neck, making the color of his eyes stand out even from across the room. The chain of his pocket watch snaked out of his breast pocket, a reminder of their time together in Avorstead.

Her sisters threw flower petals over the rest of her path, and Edward and Charles helped her up the two steps at the front until she stood directly in front of Barnaby.

"Don't mess this up," Tobie growled menacingly to Barnaby.

"We know where to find you," Edward added before they sat down near the front of the pews. Their audience seated themselves, though the music continued playing for several more measures as Barnaby lifted the veil to reveal her face.

A sheen of moisture shimmered in his eyes to match her own happiness she felt inside.

"You're crying," she murmured.

"Lords don't cry," he chuckled, only to swipe a hand across his eyes. "You are…everything I didn't think I could have."

Her mouth twitched as she produced a handkerchief from her hidden pocket and blotted her own tears. "I think it's safe to say you are everything I never dreamed I could have."

A quiet laugh escaped him as he pulled her close enough to whisper in her ear. "I cannot wait to worship every single one of your freckles."

Ivette held a gloved hand over her mouth to cover her gasp and to divert attention away from her flushed face. "Barnaby!" she hissed, but then she covered her laugh with the same hand, trying to keep it from escaping again as the music faded out and the priestess stepped forward.

She held Barnaby's loving gaze as they exchanged their vows, and then rings, followed by an unforgettable kiss. Barnaby dipped her low and the crowd cheered wildly, his three friends cheering the loudest while her sisters clapped excitedly, each wiping the tears from their faces.

When he righted her, he pulled her close enough to whisper in her ear once again. "My beautiful wife. I will cherish you till the end of time."

Emotion clogged her throat as she kissed his cheek, and then his lips. "And I will love you with my every breath." She squeezed his hand and smiled. "Always."

ABOUT THE AUTHOR

Sydney Winward is an award-winning fantasy and paranormal romance author who dabbles in the occasional historical fiction. She loves building complex worlds filled with magic, strong characters, and emotional stories that can make you laugh and cry.

Sydney is the author of the Sunlight and Shadows Series and the best-selling Bloodborn Series, and when she's not writing, she's reading, thinking about stories, or going on adventures with her children. She lives in Utah with her husband and three amazing kids.

www.sydneywinward.com